# TALES OF THE FALLEN

## BOOK I: AWAKENINGS

THIS EDITION IS LIMITED TO 300
SIGNED & NUMBERED HARDCOVERS.
THIS IS NUMBER:

136

DAVID G. BARNETT

EDWARD LEE

# TALES OF THE FALLEN

## BOOK I: AWAKENINGS

### DAVID G. BARNETT

NECRO PUBLICATIONS
2009

first edition
TALES OF THE FALLEN
BOOK 1: AWAKENINGS

all stories © 2009 David G. Barnett
cover art © 2009 Travis Anthony Soumis
interior art © 2009 Erik WIlson

this edition January 2009 © Necro Publications

book design & typesetting:
David G. Barnett / Fat Cat Design

assistant editors:
Amanda Baird • Stefan Basic • Jeff Funk • Gak
John Everson • C. Dennis Moore • Sean Woods

a Necro Publication
5139 Maxon Terrace • Sanford, FL 32771
www.necropublications.com

trade hardcover
ISBN-10: 1-889186-21-X
ISBN-13: 978-1-889186-21-4

limited edition hardcover
ISBN: 1-889186-78-3
ISBN-13: 978-1-889186-78-8

This book is also availabe in a
deluxe limited edition hardcover of 26 copies.

Printed by
Publishers' Graphics
Carol Stream, IL

This is dedicated to all of my peoples,
I give bigtime love, huggie huggie!
Bounce!


Oh, all right, let's get somewhat serious. Special hugs for the brilliant Gerard Houarner, mastermind behind Painfreak, for allowing me to play inside his creation. To Edward Lee, mentor and friend. To Charlee Jacob, whose literary genius I could never even hope to come close to with my writing.

To my boys, Stefan, Scott R., Robert N. and Sean, who got my back when I become an idiot. Scott R. for driving my drunk ass home and holding onto my belt so I wouldn't splat face first onto I-4 as I puked out his passenger window. For Stefan who at least threw a blanket on me when I passed out in the Ybor Hilton after too many of Ms. Tia's vodkas with Red Bull and shots at The Castle. To Robert N. for having even more fucked up hours than me so I have someone to play World of Warcraft with after midnight.

And finally to my lovely women that decorate my life with their beauty: Audrea, Amanda, Amy, and Angel. Why do they all have names that begin with the letter A? Weird.

And finally, to my family, who just simply rule.

# BOOK I: AWAKENINGS

## INTRODUCTION
7

## OF ANGELS FALLEN
11

## DADDY DEMON'S DAY OUT
63

## THE SLEEPERS AWAKEN
147

In a world that can often be viewed as a symbolic pile of excreta—depending on one's perspective, of course—we all need our modes of escape. Fiction serves as one such escape, and in my opinion it's the most effective, because it invites all of the participant's sensibilities, unlike, say, film, which only requires the viewer to point his or her face at the screen and pay attention, or, I suppose, drugs, which not only turns people into losers, it merely requires the induction of said drug, then you get high, then the high goes away, and you're still a loser. But the high of good fiction NEVER goes away. It's always there, long after the final page is turned, recurring to our faculties, replaying its thrill, and maintaining its invitation to provoke not just thought in general but deep, thematic, and even philosophical speculation. This is very important when one considers the sheer function of escapism; i.e. GOOD fiction gives us that very special bonus—or double-whammy: entertainment, PLUS an ethereal fulcrum, so to speak, on which we are entreated to weigh the subjective "in-betweens" of our world-view, and—dang

# INTRODUCTION

it!—the best stuff out there always seems to be negative or even nihilistic. It is my judgment, then, that the fiction that we like the most provides our avenue of escape from this enormous hock-ball of the gods—this symbolic pile of excreta—called the world, or, more broadly, the modern human condition.

Gee, Wally, isn't that pretty fuckin' cynical?

Well, yeah, Beave, I guess it fuckin' is.

Personally, cynicism doesn't suit me, or at least, I find myself growing more and more optimistic as my fifty-year-old ass trudges ever onward toward being a fifty-one-year old ass. Ultimately, however, it occurs to me that the fiction of today which offers the most mental meat to the reader is modern, cutting-edge material such as David G. Barnett's *Tales of the Fallen*. This is cynicism and then some, brothers and sisters. In fact, these three intertwining stories propose a work that may well be the Mother of All cynicism.

Think Tarantino meets John Fowles' *The Magus*, with a dash of Bosch and a shot of Count Cagliostro, all mixed up in Macbeth's cauldron and distilled down to a phantasmal mental ichor, a wild mix indeed. Populated by supernatural killing machines, snide demons, monstrous apprentices, anti-Godheads, and aspiring sorcerers, Barnett shows us the crumbling, corrupt vista of our own world made grimmer by a coal-black antithesis of spirituality. Here a trine of plots twist about our inquiring minds like Cthulhuian tentacles, only to merge into not just a singular denial of status quo religious thesis but also in a proposition of a Heaven-Hell mythos so far-reaching you'll get lost in ensuing contemplation for some time to come: a very dark wonderworld of subjective opposites which all seems to function as a character itself. If you're into literary symbolism, look harder between this book's ornaments (the staunch gore, the gritty naturalism, the belly-busting sarcasm, and a wonderful modernized M.R. James-like occult science) and you'll be left with something staring back at you darker than the visage in Nietzsche's Abyss. It's not everywhere you can find such theologic gems packed into one break-neck occult thriller.

Hmmm, perhaps this preamble is getting a bit stodgy; there seem to be more run-on sentences than, say, an M.R. James story! But I'm weary of new millennial intros/blurbs/endorsements because they all sound so colloquial. Certainly I could say, instead, "Shit-yeah, Dave Barnett's *Tales of the Fallen* kicks mucho ass, man, and it takes names! Dude, it's got all kinds of cool shit, like incarnation spells in one of those 25-cent lick-on tattoo machines, and a devil's whorehouse, and enough blood and guts to fill a fuckin' dump truck, oh, and Bunklewarts, man, which are these slick little demonic shit-bugs that live in a monster's ASS, man! Conjuration, masturbation, ejaculation, assassination, and GOD in a fuckin' diner—yowzah! It's got it all! No shit! It's the best fuckin' horror story I've read this year! Dude!"

Certainly, all of the above are quite true but, lo, such exclamatory banter is not a reflection of my style. Such a tone is too inexorably commonplace, which supports an ultimate point. Barnett's horrific ternary of words, places, and characters is anything BUT commonplace.

# INTRODUCTION

Instead, it's a unique and very refreshing vision, the perfect fruit to pluck off of horror fiction's tree for the new dark age. So? Back to stodgy run-on sentences.

Here's my favorite line in the entire book: "For what falls from your diseased and worn womb will be the salvation of us all." Ah, such exuberance! But there's a joke hidden in there—a joke on us all—because when you think hard and consider the potential symbology of that line, Barnett leaves us with the book's core truth: take the summation of what we typically want to believe and then turn it inside-out. There's our truth. An inversion more perverted and depressing than anything we can imagine. And when we look at the world of the past and the world of today—and all its escalating outrage, prevarication, and horror—it may well be that the aforementioned womb proves far more than a vessel for birth. In fact, it seems to be gestating quite well in my opinion, and is perhaps quickly approaching the end of the last trimester. Barnett, either cruelly or gleefully, forces us to envision what might come out.

In a hip style and sharp, velotic prose, Barnett has unleashed a celebration of abomination, a pallet of mythological freight right to the readership's front door. Cynicism and heresy has rarely been more provocative—or entertaining—than what you are about to read.

Edward Lee
March 23, 2008
St. Pete Beach, Florida

# OF ANGELS FALLEN

The woman's body slid down the wall as if in slow motion—too slow. Mal put his finger on the bridge of her nose and pressed down hoping to quicken the descent. When her legs finally collapsed, she crumbled into a pile at his feet—forehead resting on the cum-, piss-, what-have-you?-stained carpet. Mal put the steel-tip of his Doc Marten into her temple and gave her a quick kick. No sign of life. Of course there was no real sign of life before he shoved the seven-inch blade in one side of her skinny neck and out the other. Just because she was breathing didn't mean she was alive. Her heavy-lidded eyes had exploded at the realization that something was horribly wrong. Her left hand, which had been deftly stroking Mal's cock, gave a sharp, hard squeeze as he unloaded onto the front of her filthy, pink PVC skirt. He placed his hand on hers and squeezed to keep the pressure tight on his shaft. He kept her hand moving along his cock to work out a few more drops while she hung there in the air stunned and bleeding out. "Finish the job, honey. Always finish the job."

From the other room Mal heard her crack-head baby crying for something he wasn't going to be getting anytime soon. "Sorry, brother, momma's tapped out."

Mal dropped the knife next to the "whore" and stuffed his slick-tipped dick back into his pants. *At least with this one I got a good crank out,* he thought. *Even if I did have to finish it off myself.*

The kid wailed again, sensing something wrong in the air. Mal thought about paying him a little visit on his way out. Then shrugged it off. They would take care of him, her and everything else just like they always did. No concerns on his part. Mal's jizz, his blood, his fingerprints… Didn't matter.

Mal walked by the screaming kid's room and poked his head in. "Take it easy there, twitchy. Maybe they'll take you in and save you like they did me," he said before shooting him a quick thumbs-up and heading out the door.

«« — »»

*Balance of power*, that's what they called it. For every good, decent life extinguished at the hand of evil, retribution is needed in the name of the righteous. This is what he had been taught since they had rescued him from the gutter.

Twenty-two and already a bum—a bottle of whiskey

a day for the past year left Mal numb and free of any concerns other than where the next bottle came from. Petty theft, B&E, a little assault here and there, blood siphoned into a bottle for some poor bastard brought into an ER after Mal had just beat the shit out of him for twelve bucks and some change.

Yeah, Mal was leading the charmed life. Then one night of too much booze and too little thinking, he tried to force the wrong guy to give up his wallet. The guy was big, too big Mal would soon find out. But the alcohol and the need inside Mal made him feel as if *he* was even bigger. Mal came at the guy, stammering and wobbling, finger poking in his coat pocket pointing a cotton gun. The guy stopped but didn't seem scared, instead he just stared at Mal through black watery eyes, his head tilted slightly, his brow creased. He looked like a confused puppy trying to figure out what his owner wanted him to do.

"Give me your money, asshole. Now!" Mal screamed. Trying hard to be menacing. He puffed out his chest, trying to seem larger than he really was—larger than the stranger whom he now realized was a *hell* of a lot bigger than Mal first thought. It was a sad display.

The stranger just stood there as if studying the situation. Mal teetered on his feet and started to lean back. He blinked and when he opened his eyes no one was in front of him. Before Mal could make sense of what was going on, the bottle of bottom-shelf whiskey sitting on the ground where Mal placed it before rising to intimidate, was coming up the side of his head. The stranger's motion was lightning fast and his aim was dead on. One second Mal was starting to jack this guy, the next he's falling to the curb with a cascade of whiskey and blood covering the side of his face, then his body.

Mal hit the ground, shook his head, stunned, and rolled onto his back. Blinking manically through the whiskey-stung eyes, Mal tried to look up. The guy looked down at him, his head still tilted slightly. A flash of orange appeared before Mal's face, shadows danced for a second and in them he could see the stranger grinning—but only for a second before the grin vanished and the flame dropped down onto Mal's body. One moment he felt cold, wet and dazed. The next he was completely sober, every inch of his body awake to the sensation of excruciating pain as his whiskey-soaked coat burned away, then his shirt, then…his flesh. The screams that erupted into the night seemed distant as if Mal were hearing them from blocks away. *He wasn't on fire. He couldn't be. It had to be someone else.* Someone else in this pain. Someone else screaming into the dank air. Someone else hearing the low murmuring of voices coming from right behind the wall of flames. It had to be someone else. Not him. Not…

«« — »»

He had killed the crackhead whore because they told him to kill a hooker. Actually, they said "harlot." Guess it wasn't as crude as hooker. They're not big on the vulgar. Silly when you consider what they are big on. Whatever. Mal knew what the hell they meant.

When he got back in his car, Mal quickly noticed the package sitting on his passenger seat. He knew immediately what it was by the mark—a flaming sword, red. Mal still laughed at their lack of subtlety. "It's about fucking time," he said opening the package. What he found inside confused him. So he picked up the piece of paper. "Finally!" Mal's eyes filled with tears as he read the note another time just to make sure:

*This will be your last assignment.*
*Your reward is nigh.*

«« — »»

The sharp stink of rubbing alcohol mixed with shit assaulted Mal when he first awoke. He opened his eyes and immediately felt like someone had punched him in the face. The light seared into the back of his brain—pain attacking his skull like a jackhammer.

*Pain...*

Amidst the pounding in his head, Mal saw flashes—images—ricocheting through his mind.

*A bottle crashing into the side of his head...*
*Face against the black top of a street...*
*An orange grin...*

Then...
*... a flame ...*
*...falling ...*
*...falling.*
Mal sees himself...
*Screaming ...*
*... screaming ...*
*... through a wall of fire ...*
*... covering him in white hot pain.*

But only for a few seconds... Then only the screams remained. Mal heard them as if someone were standing next to him—mouth an inch from his ear—unleashing a banshee cry directly into his brain.

Through the screams and the incessant *thump-thump* in his head, Mal managed to feel hands on his shoulders. They pressed into him, pinning him down. He chanced opening his eyes again. This time more cautiously. A fraction of light seeped through. *A little more*, he thought, as the cold white light pried its way into his eyes.

The screams subsided, chased away by the light. The pain in Mal's head settled into just a light pulsing. He gave into the pressure against his shoulders and settled back into the pillow behind his head. He blinked a few more times, trying to focus. He saw what looked like two hairy and thick tree limbs on either side of him. A blink later he realized they were actually arms. He followed them up and thought, *Great, I'm being held down by a refrigerator with arms.*

On top of the living appliance was a head the size of a watermelon—a big fucking watermelon—with long, golden hair. Mal could have sworn he saw a glow behind the giant, golden head. Almost like a...

Mal shook his head trying to clear his blurry vision. When he looked up again, the glow had abated somewhat leaving just a large—make that very large—man in a white suit, with golden locks cascading down around his massive shoulders.

"What the fuck," was all Mal could say.

"Language, Mr. Branch. Language," came a voice from somewhere in the room. Then: "Please allow our guest some room." Mal felt the pressure on his shoulders disappear as the behemoth let go of him.

"There. That's better. Right, Mr. Branch?"

Mal shoved himself up onto his elbows trying to figure out who was talking to him. He cocked his head and looked up at the guy who had been holding him. "What's up, *corn-fed*?" he asked nodding to the big fellow. Then flinched as the guy moved, thinking he was going to shove him back down or crush him into a ball like tin foil.

"Relax, Mr. Branch. Desmond won't hurt you," said the voice again as the room suddenly became brighter. The mass of human before him moved to the left as a moon passing out of an eclipse. Where Mal first thought the guy was glowing and wasn't, there was no mistaking that the figure that appeared from behind Desmond...*was* glowing. *A lot*.

OF ANGELS FALLEN

«« — »»

*Should have realized this would be a hard one.* Mal shook his head, lips twisted in aggravation. But soon he let out a huff of slight amusement. *Fuck it. Go out with a bang, I guess.*

Mal had been watching his mark for a while now. And one thing was certain: this was no ten-dollar chickenhead whose skull he could smash into the grimy wall of a dead-end alley after the whore finished sucking him off. Nope, this one would take some planning.

Jericho White was a powerful man—a *very* powerful man: high profile and almost never alone as executive assistants and hired meat moved around in a carousel dance of top-notch ass kissing. Yep, Mal had his work cut out for him on this one.

Whores, bums, an entire cult, a busload of geriatrics from Atlantic City, dictators, even a school full of children, thousands…all training—years and years of training. Training to follow orders, to obey…to kill.

«« — »»

"It's quite simple, Mr. Branch. We would like you to work for us."

Mal tried to look directly at whatever the hell was glowing at the foot of his bed. But his eyes hadn't fully adjusted to working status again and he felt his gaze avert itself toward the floor, the ceiling, anywhere but straight ahead.

"Is there a problem, Mr. Branch?" the glow asked.

"Um… Well… You, ah, know you're all super glowy and shit, right?" Mal responded.

"Ah, yes. I do tend to forget. It's been a while since I've been around someone not used to my…condition."

"The glowy thing is a 'condition'? What fucking condition makes you do that?"

The man flinched at Mal's words. "I will make you a deal, Mr. Branch. I will hide my 'glowy thing' as you put it, *if* you promise to refrain from being profane in my presence." And the light surrounding the voice began to abate.

Mal shrugged, "Okay. I'll try, but it ain't gonna be easy. I came out of the womb middle finger in the air. Know what I mean?" he asked, trying to see what was forming at the end of his bed.

"Indeed. A lovely image. Your mother would have been quite proud—"

"Yeah, well—"

"—provided she had lived. Right, Mr. Branch?"

Mal laid there, mouth agape, hands twitching. *This is fucked up*, he thought. *How the hell…*

"How did I know your mother died while unleashing you unto this world?"

"Uhh…" was all Mal could dribble out of his mouth. His vision began to clear and he found he could look straight ahead finally. A man stood before him. A man like no other Mal had ever seen. He stood at least seven feet tall—easily as tall as the Desmond guy, but not as wide. Tall, slim, almost wispy…yet…his ice blue eyes locked onto Mal's eyes and as Mal stared deep into them, he felt a power, an electricity that flowed directly from this man into his veins. And Mal knew instantly that this was no ordinary man…and this was no ordinary situation… Mal was lost, swimming in the man's eyes, feeling the hairs on his skin stand up. He felt as though his tether to his world had been snapped and he was floating loose, out of control toward infinity. He had no idea where he was, what he was doing, where he would go, but he knew that whatever happened, this man would be the one to lead him. He felt the man's voice wrap around him—a warm blanket with Mal nestled deep within.

"Mr. Branch?"

"Uhmm…" Mal shook his head, trying to get back to reality.

"We have much to discuss, Mr. Branch."

"Call me Mal…"

"Alright…Mal. Let's get you fed and dressed. Desmond is here for you. I'll leave you for now and when you are ready, he will bring you to me."

Mal felt an enormous shadow fall over his left side as Desmond reached out and lowered the safety rail on Mal's bed, the metallic *clank* shattering the serenity of the room, bringing Mal fully back to his senses.

"Uh… Okay," Mal managed as he swung his legs over the side of the bed. He felt Desmond's big hands grab his arm to offer support as he tried to stand. "Who are you, by the way?" Mal asked, turning his head to the end of the bed, which now held nothing but emptiness.

Mal shook his head again, "Ooookay. Guess that comes later, huh, big guy."

Desmond said nothing and proceeded to lift Mal to his feet. He felt like a newborn foal standing for the first time. But he quickly got his legs underneath him. He had questions that needed answering. Something told him things were going to be very different from now on. Very…*very*…different.

Mal had never really stressed about assignments before. Sure, at the beginning, but that had been so long ago. The jobs, like the years, ran together. Most of them required very little planning. Mostly off-the-cuff dealings. Mal was never really worried. He knew his tracks would be covered. Plus, he was blessed. How could anything go wrong, ever? But something told Mal he needed to focus some more on this job. After all, it was his last. And after all these years, the brass ring was in sight. Time to grab it and get off the ride.

Mal tried to simplify things, break it down to the bare bones. Jericho White lived in one building, worked in another. He ate at restaurants and shopped in stores, of course they were all topnotch places, but still… Jericho White was just a man when you broke it down. But it wasn't as simple as that. Something deep down in his gut gnawed at Mal, telling him that this was different. But for some reason he couldn't figure out exactly what it was.

Mal had gone after many men. All were the same. You find their weakness, expose it, and take advantage of their vulnerability. In Mal's wake you could have followed the trail of dead bodyguards that led from the lobby to the seventieth floor of one of Japan's highest-security buildings. At the end of the body trail you'd find Sado Hiroki, head general of the Japanese Yakuza, strung up by his ankles above his desk, a pool of blood collecting on his leather blotter, his skin—expertly flayed by one of his prized Samurai swords—situated in his $5000 chair, clothed in his $10,000, hand-tailored suit looking like nothing more than a deflated blow-up doll.

Follow Mal's path again, this time deep into the heart of the South American rainforest and you'd find an entire village of guerilla soldiers sitting motionless, side-by-side, forming a perfect circle around a campfire—a little odd at first glance. But as you moved closer, you'd sense that something was more than just a *little* odd here. Approach further and find a helium-filled balloon pinned to the collar of every headless neck, and a goofy face magic-markered onto the smooth rubber.

And as you look down, you see each man's head positioned between their own legs, neck in the dirt crawling with ants, lids pinned open, eyes reflecting the fire as their cocks—expertly separated from their bodies—turned to ash inside the dancing flames.

Mal was a master assassin. A man with the God-given skills to cause murder and mayhem wherever he was told to go and sometimes even when he wasn't told to. The skills had always been there, but it took some work to bring them out after they had been buried beneath years of general malaise and apathy followed by a substantial stint of substance abuse.

«« — »»

"You want me to do *what*?" Mal said incredulously.

"You are to go into the school. Find room 315. Enter. Then dispense with the teacher. A Mrs. Sally Burnsfield." Desmond looked down at Mal, his green eyes showing no emotion.

Mal stared out from their hiding place next to the utility building on the edge of school grounds.

"Why?" he asked shaking his head, not comprehending the order.

*Crack!*

Mal flew backwards, back smashing hard into brick. The hand struck his face like a bolt of lightning; it hit hard and fast…and it burned. Mal collapsed into a heap next to the building, resting his burning cheek on the cool autumn grass.

"Jesus-fucking-Christ, Desi."

In one swift motion, Desmond reached down, grabbed Mal by his ankle and lifted him up. Mal dangled limp from the giant's grip. Desmond continued to stare at the school—no sweat, no emotion—a cold, solid statue of a man. Mal tried to get his bearings.

"What have I told you, Mr. Branch, about taking the Lord's name in vain?"

"Don't?"

"And what have I said about calling me Desi?"

"You're not too fond of it."

"Then why do you persist in pushing my ire, Mr. Branch?" Desmond asked. Then he dropped Mal on his head.

Mal scrambled upright and pushed his back up against the wall and sat there shaking the stars from his eyes. "It's what I do, man. I'm a smart ass. It's my shtick. Lighten up."

"It is not my *duty* to lighten up, Mr. Branch. It is my *duty* to make sure you are trained properly. It is my *duty* to give you assignments *and* it is my *duty* to make sure your *true talents* come to the surface. You are weak and sloppy and my patience is growing weary. So, please, Mr. Branch, save your 'shtick' for the whores and scum with which you choose to surround yourself when not in my presence." Desmond finally stopped looking at the school, yet maintained his cool demeanor, which Mal was sure was even more threatening than if he was being yelled at. "Every time you decide to be funny with me I will hit you. And believe me when I tell you, Mr. Branch, I will hit you harder each time. I will break you of this need to push me. You will learn discipline…or you will *be* disciplined."

Mal stared into Desmond's eyes and tried with all his might not to piss in his pants.

"Are we perfectly clear, Mr. Branch?"

"Crystal."

Desmond leaned down and put his face only inches from Mal's. "And what is my name, Mr. Branch?"

Mal slumped, not able to look into Desmond's cold black eyes anymore. "Desmond. Your name is Desmond, not Desi."

"Very good, Mr. Branch." Desmond straightened to his full height again and returned his gaze to the school. "Now, what exactly are you going to do, Mr. Branch?"

Mal pushed himself up the wall until he was standing. He tried hard not to shake. "I… I will go into the school. Find room 315. Enter. Then dispense with the teacher. A Mrs. Sally Burnsfield."

"Very good, Mr. Branch. And from now on when I give you an order what will you *not* do?" Desmond asked flatly.

"Ask why," Mal said softly.

"Excellent, Mr. Branch. Now, if you would, please

go about your task. And make sure the classroom has children in it. Do not hurt them though. We would like for them all to remember this for a very long time."

Mal wanted to turn around and walk away. He had been training for what seemed like years. Desmond showed him how to use an arsenal of various weapons. Other men were brought in to teach him how to fight. He was taught the differences between dozens of poisons. He had been taught munitions and explosives. Some Asian guys were brought in to teach Mal what he called "all that Grasshopper bullshit" and they had trained him well. He learned quickly because it was all in him already. It just needed to be extracted. And now it was time for Mal to start using all the skills he had honed, all the knowledge he had attained. He knew he would have to kill. They told him that up front. But he thought it would be someone bad: a crime lord, a dictator or something like that. Not a teacher. And why kill her in front of kids? *What the fuck?* he thought. *Can I do this?* Then Mal thought about his old life: the drugs, the alcohol, laying in a gutter covered in his own piss and vomit, people ignoring him like he was nothing more than a fire hydrant. That's when he remembered that he hated people. People sucked. So fuck it. Why worry about this one bitch? She must have done something bad. Everybody has something bad they've done, *right?* This chick must have some scary skeletons in her closet. *So...* If they wanted her dead, then she dies. After all, they had saved him. They pulled him from the gutter and washed the filth off of him and trained him to be a killer. And he had never felt more alive. He felt like he finally had a purpose—too late to try and have a conscience now. He had made the deal. He couldn't question, he couldn't doubt— not with what they were offering in the end. He just *had* to believe.

«« — »»

"We're concerned with how long it is taking you to complete your final assignment, Mr. Branch."

Mal was a little worried. They had never said anything to him before about his assignments. They just gave them to him and let him go. But he supposed that they were right this time. It had taken him a while so far. He still wasn't sure how to get to this guy. And for some reason he didn't know why. He'd gone after people just as big, just as protected. Yet, this was different. He had a bad feeling deep down about this one.

"Well, Mr. Branch?"

This was the first time Mal had seen Gregory since he had agreed to *work* for the man. Desmond had been there every day of his recovery, as had many others. And even though Mal knew his orders came directly from Gregory, the man had never shown his face again in all the years…how many years now… *Christ,* Mal thought, *I have no idea how long I've been doing this.*

He looked at Gregory and could sense a tension in him that didn't fit the man at all. Gregory seemed a little on edge and it came through in his voice. But suddenly, as if he realized Mal was sizing him up, Gregory seemed to relax and waved his hand in the air. "I can understand your apprehension. Jericho White is a powerful man— probably one of the most successful businessmen in history. His security is top notch. Plus, by all accounts he's one of the most giving of the richest people in the world. His charity seems to hold no bounds."

"I've killed a lot of people who weren't bad," Mal said, turning to look out the window of his thirtieth-floor apartment.

Gregory stood motionless for a minute just staring at Mal. Then he said, "I was curious to see how you would approach this assignment. It is a difficult one and one that will become only more so as you get closer to the man."

Gregory paused waiting for Mal to turn around. He didn't. So Gregory continued, "When the time comes, use what we gave you in the package to dispatch Mr. White. We went through a lot of effort to procure that particular item for you. He will understand the meaning and it will make the death that much sweeter for all of us."

Mal seemed to be ignoring Gregory completely. And Gregory decided not to push him. In the end he knew Mal would do his job. Because in the end what he had offered Mal for his years of service was more than enough motivation. "Remember, Mr. Branch, finish this job and our deal is complete."

"No it isn't," Mal said coldly. "I finish this job, you still have something to give me."

Gregory let out a little laugh. "Indeed, you are right. I will keep my end of the bargain. Good luck to you, Mr. Br— Mal."

And with that Gregory was gone. Mal didn't hear a rustle of clothes, didn't hear a door. He just knew that no one stood behind him anymore. And he also knew he was screwed because none of them—Gregory, Desmond, anyone working with them—had called him Mal, at least not since that day he first met Gregory. The same day he awoke to a new life, a new purpose and a signed contract for eternal salvation.

«« — »»

Mal continued staring out at the city for a long time after Gregory had disappeared. In the years since he had penned the deal with Gregory to become his hired assassin, Mal had come to feel like he owned this city. He could come and go as he pleased. He could do what he wanted to whatever or whomever he wanted and just walk away. He had brought death to hundreds, maybe thousands, he didn't know anymore. He was chaos thrown into chaos. It was what he was born to do. He knew this now. Had known it since that first kill, the teacher. *What was her name…*

# OF ANGELS FALLEN

«« — »»

Mal had approached the school slowly. His nerves were frayed. He was shaking. Sweating. He did as he was told, though. He found room 315 and looked into the small glass window criss-crossed with wire mesh. Inside the room stood a small woman, hair pulled back into a tight bun, tiny glasses slipped slightly down her cute, upturned nose. She was leaning back against the front of her desk as she stared down her glasses into a book. Mal could see her lips moving, and through the door he could hear a slight murmur as her voice brought to life the fantasy winter world that lay beyond the back of a wardrobe. The students were enthralled by the adventures of young children, like themselves, and of a powerful lion. They grew to hate the witch as they learned the difference between a hero and a villain—between good and evil.

And as Mal watched the teacher lick her finger and turn a page in the book, he felt his hand slowly reach out, grab the doorknob and turn it. He did it so quietly that no one in the class even noticed him enter the room until he was almost in. No one looked concerned, no one screamed. This was another time when fears didn't run rampant through the minds of everyone—a time when villains were on TV and in the movies and nestled deep within the pages of a book. Evil was a witch that gave small boys Turkish Delight. At least for those children it was…until that day.

Only minutes before, the last thing Mal wanted to do was kill this woman. But as he watched her through the window he felt something take over his body, his mind. He remembered watching her read and the next thing he knew he was behind her, hand over her mouth and knife to her throat. Then the screams followed. They were deafening and assaulted his senses and sent him into motion. He sliced the knife deep and fast across Mrs. Burnsfield's pale white throat. And as the blood sprayed, hot and fast across the first couple of kids sitting in the front off the class, all the sounds around him disappeared. Instead of the assault of fourth-grader screams Mal heard pure silence. It was the most beautiful sound he had ever heard. He looked out at the students, all scrambling to get away from the big bad man that just hurt their teacher. *Where was the talking lion? Where was the hero?* And for all the commotion and mouths open, straining to release the loudest screams possible, Mal heard nothing. He felt the warm blood from the now dead Mrs. Burnsfield run down his arms and meld with his flesh. And for the first time in his life Mal felt…peace. Bringing death had brought Mal…peace.

Was this a taste of what Gregory had promised him? Because if it was, and it was *only* a taste, then he would continue to do this until his time had come and he was able to walk into the warm embrace of eternal salvation—into pure bliss.

OF ANGELS FALLEN

«« — »»

One thing Mal prided himself on was the ability to not be seen. He had become one "stealthy ass mother fucker" as he liked to call himself. He could slip into anywhere unnoticed if he wanted. But sometimes it was just as easy to walk right into a place like you knew what the hell you were doing. So that's what Mal figured was the best way to get into White's building. He put on a $4000 Armani suit, slipped into some serious power shoes, put a black leather briefcase with real gold trim in his hand and walked right into the main lobby. When stopped by the guard at the front desk, Mal had simply said he had a late appointment with some stock brokerage company on the tenth floor. Which he did, he had made the appointment the day before stating he wanted to diversify his portfolio, blah, blah and was ready to funnel some serious "cashola" through the greedy hands of Hammerin, Sikes or Maskovicz. Didn't matter which one because he wasn't planning on keeping his meeting.

The guard verified the appointment with someone at the brokerage company and pointed Mal to the large array of elevators across the lobby. Mal said thanks and headed toward them, boarded one and got off on the tenth floor where he met a cheerful receptionist tethered to a huge half-circle desk by a headset. Mal made a show of getting a phone call. He peppered the fake conversation with "nows" and "you're kiddings" and ended with an "oh, alright, I'll be there in a couple" followed by a heart-felt apology to the receptionist and a promise of a call tomorrow to reschedule. And within seconds Mal was out of the door heading back toward the elevator. The receptionist had turned back to answer a call and didn't see that Mal wasn't heading to the lobby, but was in fact heading up, up and up to the fiftieth floor—to Jericho White's office.

While in the elevator, Mal pulled a Mac-10 from his briefcase. It was given to him by one of his instructors and was his favorite for infiltration where there would be a number of people in his way. It held 32 rounds and was fast and efficient. He used it to kill the same instructor two years later. He found it poetic; he wondered if the instructor found it *poetic* as well just before a bullet exploded through his head.

Mal's plan was simple—when the elevator door slid open he'd shoot whoever was between him and White. It was a brutish plan, it lacked subtlety, but he wanted it that way. It was his last assignment and he wanted to have some fun at least.

Mal took a deep breath as he reached the 49th floor and let it out slowly as the red digital numbers changed to 50. He braced himself, pointed the gun ahead of him and waited for the doors to slide open. Someone would be getting a big surprise once they did.

A bell sounded, Mal waited, his finger twitched on

the trigger, the doors slid open and Mal stepped into the offices of Jericho White and came face-to-face with…

…nothing.

He was shocked by the lack of life. He had prepared to kill and there was nothing to kill. He felt betrayed. He felt hollow, unfulfilled inside, like a child ripping into a present at Christmas only to find socks and not the toy he desired so much.

Before him was a typical office waiting area—professionally decorated but maintaining a warm *welcome* feel. Mal moved to the receptionist's area and took a look behind it. Abandoned. His eyes fell over the counter, what lay behind it looked like it hadn't been touched in a while. A fine layer of dust had settled over the black counter and everything else. His eyes moved back and forth and settled on the phone…

*riinnggg riinnggg*

For the first time in a long while Mal jumped. More like a twitch to most people, but to Mal it was one step away from pissing himself.

*riinnggg riinnggg*

He hesitated for a second, then reached over the counter and picked up the phone.

"Mr. Branch. Welcome. Won't you please join me? Follow the corridor to the office at the end."

Mal nodded as if he knew he was being watched.

"Oh, and Mr. Branch. Don't worry about anyone trying to stop you. I assure you, it's just you and me here."

Mal heard the line go dead. He placed the phone back in its cradle and turned. Ahead of him stretched a corridor of doors. All the same—all closed. Mal should move down the hall slowly, but something told him he was safe—for now at least. He picked up his pace and approached the door at the end of the hall. This door was different than the rest. It spanned at least ten feet across, constructed of dark, heavy, hard wood. The handles where made of gold. They fanned out, one on each door, forming the shape of wings. Mal reached for the handles but stopped and opted instead to push the door open with his gun. Both doors swung open easily and wide. Mal stepped into the office of Jericho White, his gun leading the way like it had so many times before.

Mal heard the voice from the phone once again. "Mr. Branch, welcome." The voice seemed to come from all around. He spun, trying to find its source.

"It's okay, Mr. Branch. I'm right here."

And a shadow came to life directly in front of Mal in the form of Jericho White. Mal leveled the gun at White's chest.

"So, Mr. Branch. I understand you've come to kill me."

Mal tried to pull himself together and gave a nonchalant shrug, the gun never moving.

White smiled and leaned back against his massive desk, unconcerned about the weapon aimed at his heart.

*Who the Hell needs a desk that fucking big?* Mal wondered.

"A powerful man," White said flatly.

Mal squinted as though in pain. "Okay, you know what? Stay out of my fucking head, alright? I mean, seriously, I hate that," Mal said through clenched teeth. "Gre…"

White's eyebrows went up in mock surprise. "What is it, Mal? Can I call you Mal?"

Mal shrugged again. "Sure. Let's be casual… Jerry."

White let loose a big smile, amused at Mal's cockiness. "Please finish. Gre…? Greg…? Gregory? I know perfectly well it was Gregory who sent you to kill me, Mal."

Somehow, Mal wasn't surprised White knew this. He was getting the distinct impression he was caught in the middle of some game. And this sudden revelation was starting to seriously piss him off.

"Gregory likes to get inside people's heads. We all do really. It's a natural ability. It can be controlled though. Although I doubt Gregory is showing much restraint these days. Never has been able to control his power. Loose cannon as they say."

Mal went along. "Oh yeah. You and Greg ole buddies?"

White crossed his arms over his chest, nodding at the same time. "You could say that."

"Let me guess. Old business partners? One stabbed the other in the back and now this has been years in the works. Old Greg finally getting the upper hand by sending me in to finish off the competition?"

White shook his head. "Well, if you'd like to put it in such banal terms. Fine, yes, a bad deal. But it really is so much more than that, Mal." White stood up and moved his arms dramatically as if pointing out pictures on the wall. "It's a timeless tale. One of deceit and treachery. Of murder and jealousy. All the good stuff of classic drama. Shakespeare couldn't have penned a better tale."

"Oh yeah. So who are you in this story? The treacherous villain soon to get what's coming to him or the tragic hero?" Mal asked.

White settled down, thinking about Mal's question. "Hmmm. A little of both I suppose. Depends on who you speak to…" White hesitated. "…you think you could put your gun away, Mal?"

"Probably not."

"It's kind of rude at this point."

Mal smirked. "Not exactly Miss Manners here, Jerry."

White shrugged. "Well, I asked nicely…"

Light exploded from around White's body, reaching out toward Mal. Mal instinctively fired six quick rounds directly into White's chest. And just as suddenly as the light shot forward it retreated, leaving nothing but silence and the smell of gunpowder hanging in the air.

Mal blinked his eyes back into working and six dark holes dotting White's chest. Yet White continued to stand there, taking in Mal with his now golden eyes.

"Hmm. Neat trick."

"Need I ask again?"

"Suppose not," Mal lamented, lowering the gun and then quickly stowing it inside his jacket. And just as quickly pulling something else out. For the first time since being in White's presence Mal sensed a change in the man's demeanor. White's cool confidence had disappeared, replaced instead with a definite uneasiness. His eyes locked onto the object in Mal's hand.

Mal was a little surprised by White's reaction. But relieved just the same. For the first time since walking into this office, Mal finally felt slightly more in control. "What's a'matter, Jer? Seen a ghost or something?"

White's eyes became slits as he tried to regain some composure. "You could say that."

"Little gift—"

"From your master, no doubt?" White said through clenched teeth.

"Yep. That Gregory… He's a giver."

White gave a disgusted grunt. "He's a fool."

"Careful, there, Jer… Wouldn't want to go getting me all upset by calling Gregory names. He is my—"

"Your what?" White interrupted. His eyes had changed, the whites disappearing, buried under an intense glow of gold.

This startled Mal a little. "I'd go ahead and calm down a bit, Jerry. The eye thing…makes me twitchy. Bad things could happen if I get too twitchy. So save the theatrics and tricks for someone else."

White sighed. "Fine. Is this what you want?" White asked as his eyes returned to normal. He followed this with a shake of his head. "Ironic," he said, amused.

"What's funny, Jerry? I like a good joke."

"This..." White motioned up and down his body with a wave of his hand. "...*this* is the trick. This is what you want to believe is real. But you know don't you, Mal?"

"Know what?"

"That all this is a façade. You just refuse to admit it to yourself. You know what this is. You know what I am, what Gregory is."

Mal hesitated, then shot White a quick nod. "Maybe."

White moved to his chair behind his desk and sat, crossing his hands on the desktop and leaning in as if ready to negotiate.

"What is your reward? What has Gregory offered you for your years of service—your years of sin against humanity?"

Mal paused for a brief second, then simply said...

«« — »»

"Salvation."

Mal was confused. What the Hell was this guy talking about? Salvation? How can you offer someone *salvation?* Besides, Mal was pretty sure he was beyond being saved at this point—

"No one is beyond being saved, Mr. Branch," replied Gregory, interrupting Mal's thoughts.

Mal frowned. "Seriously, man. Knock that crap off."

Gregory gave a short, quick apologetic nod. "Forgive me. Sometimes my manners falter."

"Yeah, well…" Mal's mind was already off the subject. He returned to the offer.

"Let me assure you that I can certainly deliver on my promises, Mr. Branch."

Mal's doubt showed on his face. He looked at the flesh mountain to his left, but got no help from Desmond whatsoever.

This was his decision—no one here to help him.

"Do you doubt my power to deliver you into the arms of salvation, Mr. Branch?"

"Well, come on, Greg. Seriously. Turn on the radio and you can hear a dozen fast-talkin' Bible thumpers offering to save you." Mal shrugged. "What makes you so special?"

Gregory's intense stare bored into him. "Do you remember what it was like that last night before you awoke unto me?"

The corner of Mal's left eye twitched ever so slightly as the memory hit him. He struggled to remain in control and managed to pull off a strained shrug. "Little warm," he said nonchalantly.

Gregory's stare softened. "A master of the cool understatement."

"Yeah, well, that which does not kill us... And all that."

"Oh, but it did kill you, Mal."

Mal bristled.

"But it was me that pulled you away from death's embrace and an eternity of damnation," Gregory stated flatly.

"Praise the Lord!" Mal exclaimed.

Gregory stood quickly, and in a flash Mal was flying sideways off his chair.

"You will not speak light of the Lord." Gregory's anger pulsed with white hot heat like the hand mark on the side of Mal's face.

"Fu..." Mal started to swear before thinking better of it. "Man, Greg. Not a fan of the touchy feely. Know what I mean?" He struggled to shake the stars from his vision.

"It is my belief that subtlety and gentle suggestion fail to work on you, Mal. You fancy yourself a tough man. Well, then I will show you I am tougher."

"No need. I get it."

"Now, just so you remember the roles here... A little reminder of what you were saved from..." Gregory gave a slight wave of his hand and Mal found himself on the floor writhing in sheer agony as he felt invisible flames engulf his body.

Gregory raised his voice over Mal's screams of anguish. "It was *I* who saved you from this pain before.

It was *I* who pulled you from an *eternity* of such pain and suffering. And it is *I* and *I* alone who offers you salvation."

Another quick wave of his hand and the phantom fire disappeared. But Mal continued to scream, his body shaking violently, his eyes going wide and glassy as he rapidly approached shock. Gregory leaned down to within an inch of Mal's face. "Salvation," he said quietly and lightly placed his fingers upon Mal's brow. Mal's shaking ceased, as did his screams. He lay there looking up into Gregory's golden eyes—deep into the eyes of...his savior.

«« — »»

"All premeditated to manipulate you into his service," White said with a sigh.

Mal heard White's voice as if it were in the distance. And he snapped out of his memories and locked eyes with White. "Oh yeah? How so?"

"If you will allow me, I can show you what happened that night."

"You want in my head don't you?"

White shook his head. "Not at all. I invite you into my memories and the memories of those who work with me."

"Yeah, but still, what happens to my body while we take a trip down *your* memory lane? Don't really want to wake up naked on the side of the road with a twenty taped to my forehead and my asshole bleeding."

White frowned. "You are a crude man, Mr. Branch."

Mal shrugged. "Yeah, well, you know… No momma raising me and all that. No manners…"

"No excuses…"

Mal shrugged again. "Oh…so I'm not allowed to play the no-mommy card like every other pathetic fucker in the world? That doesn't seem fair."

"Would you like to see your mother, Mr. Branch?"

"Uh," Mal was stunned by the offer. He started to say something smart-ass, but instead stumbled on his words. He eventually got something out. "You knew my mother?"

"Knew?" White shook his head. "No. But I was… aware of her. Just as *Gregory* keeps an eye on everything I do, I keep a keen eye trained on him at all times."

Mal mulled it over for a few seconds. "So you promise me no hanky-panky while we do this?"

"My word that nothing will happen to you. I am simply not allowed to harm you."

"Why is it I believe you?"

White just stared at him.

"Okay. Let's do this then, " Mal relented.

White's eyes turned gold again and Mal felt a slight rustling of the air around him. A moment later he was standing in an alley in a shitty part of town. Shitty, and familiar. He looked out of the alley entrance at the scene unfolding across the street. Mal didn't want to admit it, but he knew what he was seeing. A skinny little rat of a guy was stumbling up to a mountain of a man—a huge man with long, golden hair. And Mal knew instantly that he had been played because there was no doubt just who the guy was…Desmond.

The scene continued to play out and it wasn't exactly what Mal remembered. His old, drunk self was a disaster on two feet. He approached the huge man in a barely controlled lurch. Mal could hear his old crackling voice break through the silent air—the words slurred and almost incomprehensible. But Mal knew what his ghost was saying. And he cringed. Then he watched the blur that was Desmond slide behind the old Mal and hit him upside the head with the bottle. Then Mal watched as Desmond lit a match and dropped it onto the bloody, crumpled pile on the ground. And even though he couldn't feel the flames, a long suppressed memory resurfaced and Mal felt sick.

That sick feeling grew more intense as he saw another figure suddenly appear out of the shadows and come up next to Desmond. Mal watched as Gregory looked down upon the burning body. He waved his hand and the flames disappeared. Mal saw Gregory say something to Desmond before the giant removed his coat and laid it on top of Mal's charred body. Desmond picked up what was left of Mal, cradling it like a baby, and walked off into the shadows behind Gregory.

Another sensation of wind swirling around him and

Mal quickly found himself standing in dark shadows once again. Only this time it was in an even shittier place than where he had just relived being burned to death. The smell hit him first: garbage, shit, piss, rotting flesh, disease and despair. The stench attacked his senses, sending his stomach into convulsions. He struggled to not vomit and eventually won.

Mal's eyes began to adjust to the dim light. Sounds rose up around him. But one sound quickly drowned out all others. Like someone turning the knob up slowly on a radio, the scream built to a crescendo. Mal winced and focused on where the sound had come from. And there on the ground, naked from the waist down, lay a woman in a small puddle of filthy water. Her legs spread wide, her thighs coated with blood and the head of a baby sticking out of her tearing vagina. "Help me!" she screamed.

For a split second Mal thought she was screaming for him, then he heard an all too familiar voice. Mal peered into the deep shadows and saw him…his savior…standing away from the woman, watching with a look of complete disgust etched into his perfect face.

"You need no help, whore. You are an animal. You are one of the *blessed* ones. You were given life and free will. You have taken this glorious gift from our father and wasted it by polluting your body and living like a pig wallowing in filth."

"You fucker!" the woman screamed and managed to hock up a good wad of spit and fired it at Gregory.

"Gutter trash."

"This is your goddamn baby, you bastard. Fucking help…" And she let loose another soul-shattering scream. Mal watched as the baby slid another inch into the world. And he felt sick because he knew damn well who that baby was to become.

"True, whore. It *is* my child. And you shall die knowing that the only good and sacred thing you have done in your miserable existence is be the vessel for my son. For what falls from your diseased and worn womb is the salvation for us all."

Gregory stepped out of the shadows and raised his arms. Light formed around him and grew to such an intensity that Mal had to look away. Gregory's voice grew as loud as the light was intense. And the walls of the sewer shook. His voice drowned out the woman's scream as she pushed one more time, dropping her child into the bloody puddle beneath her.

"You birth the Savior, whore. My son will rise up and become a God among men. He will be my vengeance on you pathetic animals. He will be the embodiment of chaos, for he is of me. And I am Abadon. I am chaos."

The light abated and Mal looked upon the scene of his birth. His infant self lay wailing between the sprawled legs of his mother. Blood flowed from her, bathing the baby in gore.

A shadow from behind Gregory quickly became

Desmond. He reached down and a sudden flick of his wrist and a flash of cold metal severed the child from its mother forever. Another flash and the knife was gone and Desmond deftly tied off the umbilical cord. He laid his coat over one arm, picked up the baby Mal and nestled the infant into the coat. Mal watched himself disappear into Desmond's massive embrace.

Gregory looked upon the woman.

"Please, help me," she pleaded weakly, her life quickly running out between her legs.

"Rest easy knowing that you have finally done something of purpose with your wasted life. You have brought unto this world a glorious new light. My son will clear the path for me to re-enter my kingdom, my home. My imprisonment on the festering cesspool reaches its final days. Soon I will step through the gates and claim my rightful place in Heaven. And woe be to any of my brothers who attempt to block my way. For my son will deliver them pain and suffering and they will soon learn they are not as immortal as they once thought."

And with that, Gregory stepped back into darkness and was gone. And Mal watched stunned as his mother gasped her last breath. Mal wanted to reach out to her, to hold her, to comfort her. But all he could do was stare at her still body as it lay in an ocean of blood and tears…cold and alone.

# OF ANGELS FALLEN

«« — »»

Yet another swirling sensation and Mal found himself standing in White's office once again, the image of his mother dying still reflected in his eyes. He stood there in stunned silence for a while. White waited patiently.

Finally, "Angels?"

"Yes."

"You're telling me you're all angels?"

White nodded, "Of course Mal, you know this. You've always known this. How else could Gregory have promised you salvation?"

"I suppose. But having it laid out there like that…"

"I know. The brutal truth of it all — angels are real, demons are real. Good and evil exist and there is a God."

"And what side are you on?" Mal asked with a little more than a hint of venom in his voice.

"What do you think?"

"You knew what was happening and you let it," Mal said, his jaw tight, his shoulders tensing.

White took a second to respond as if he was choosing his words carefully. "I am not allowed to interfere, Mal. None of us are."

"Bullshit!"

White sighed.

"You're an angel. Gregory is an angel. Gregory interfered."

"True," White conceded. "Gregory has lost his faith. He now exists for one goal and one goal only, to reclaim his place in heaven. And he has broken the rules to make sure this happens."

"So now he's evil?"

"It's not as simple as that."

"Why? He hurt me, seduced and got my mother pregnant, and then watched her die while laughing at her. He made me an assassin, sent me to kill countless people. It may not have been his hands that did the killing but there's still blood on them." Mal, paused, thoughts bouncing around in his head.

"Gregory has been hurt by what he sees as our father abandoning us. I truly think he just wants our father to forgive him. But like I said, he has grown impatient. It's like any child seeking the attention of its father. I feel that Gregory thinks that going through this effort, working his way back to Heaven, will show our father how much he has suffered and paid for his previous decisions."

"Kinda fucked up, huh?"

"Perhaps. But Gregory is misguided. His plans are born of frustration and desperation. We all have our roles and most of us chose to remain true to them. Others not."

Mal nodded quickly. "Yeah, that's another thing. Why the fuck are you here anyway? Shouldn't you either be in heaven playing a harp, dancing on clouds or down in hell torturing lost souls or something?"

White shrugged. "Like I said, it's not as simple as

that. The war in heaven was complicated. There were those who chose no side. Those who decided it best to stay away and let things fall where they would. Gregory was one such angel. Those who took up no arms in either defense or opposition to heaven were banished by God to this plane as punishment. Free of the torments and shame of Hell but denied the glory of Heaven. But in that punishment there was always hope that God would find forgiveness for his lost children and allow them to come home. Allow them back into the presence of his glory."

"Guess that didn't happen?"

"Being immortal can be a curse for some. Especially the impatient. Gregory and his abandoned brethren have been here for millennia upon millennia. Before man and beast. For some it has been *too* long. And they feel it is time to take matters into their own hands."

"And I am the solution to their problems," Mal said coldly.

White looked into Mal's eyes, and he saw the pain of betrayal and beyond that he saw something else. Deep into Mal's eyes there was…defeat. But then, Mal blinked and all of that was gone from his eyes, replaced by seething anger and a rage. White could feel heat rising from Mal's body and he took a step back.

Mal noticed White's reaction and cocked his head, curious. "What's wrong, Jer? See something you don't like?" And Mal remembered the last time White had been uneasy with him—a few minutes ago when he pulled the *gift* from Gregory out of his jacket.

"Let me ask you something, Jer." And Mal swiftly produced the knife once again. "You seem to be a little concerned about my little friend here." Mal could have sworn he saw White wince. But he soon regained his composure.

"You don't know what it is you hold."

"Why don't you enlighten me then."

White tried hard to seem at ease, but it was obvious he wasn't. Mal wondered if Angels could sweat.

"Do you feel the energy coursing through your weapon, Mal?"

Mal hadn't really noticed it before, but White was right, there was a definite feeling of power that came from holding the weapon. "Now that you mention it, yeah, I do."

"The war for Heaven was a brutal and violent one. Our powers aside, the battles often came down to a bloodrage frenzy of weapons and fists. Many an angel died by the blade. Our weapons were things of beauty crafted by one of our most prized artisans. During the war he and his apprentices forged weapons of immense power. An endless supply of weapons poured from their hands. But none so great as The Arsenal of Undoing. It was with these weapons that Lucifer and his followers were cast down into the pit."

Mal looked down at the knife in his hand. It was

indeed a thing of beauty. Never had he felt so in tune with a weapon before. It seemed to tap right into his soul. It knew what he wanted to do before he did. As he started to test its weight, tossing it from one hand to the other, Mal could feel the blade becoming part of him. As if it sensed the aspect of him that was of Heaven. It was the perfect weapon. Somewhere in the distance he could hear White speaking.

"What you have there is The Blade of Undoing. Forged from the essence of Heaven. Created from the substance of creation itself." White paused staring at the blade as if it were an animal about to attack. "It has the power to undo those born of Heaven."

Mal caught the last part of what White had said. "No shit?"

White nodded his head.

"So this is an angel killer. Man, that's some serious mojo."

"The weapons were supposed to be gathered and destroyed. I had always doubted they would *all* be found. Seems my fears were well founded. I'm sure one of my brothers cast into the pit stole away with a few. My guess is Gregory has made a pact with one for the weapon. Or just simply destroyed them for it."

White stopped speaking for an instant. He shook his head while looking at Mal, his eyes almost pleading. "It's a power not meant to be in mortal hands."

Mal shrugged. "I suppose not." Then he stopped

playing with the blade and looked at White with cold menace. "But then again, I'm apparently not a normal mortal am I?"

White stiffened and glared at Mal unflinching. "No, Mal. It would appear not."

Mal held his stare with White for a couple of seconds then let a smile fill his face. "Looks like I need to pay my benefactor a little visit. Maybe introduce him to the wrong end of my little buddy here."

"Or you could just walk away, Mal."

Mal started shaking his head vigorously. "No, Jer. I think you know I can't do that."

"It is a shame then."

"Yeah, I suck. But so does everyone, even those who shouldn't…like angels."

"Everything is flawed."

"Yeah, Gregory certainly is."

"Gregory is misguided, Mal. Walk away and show him all his plans were for nothing and he will be defeated." White spread his arms wide. "The world is yours, Mal. You could do the right thing."

"Yeah, I could. But where is the fun in that?"

White sighed.

"Aw, what's the matter, Jer, disappointed?"

"I have counseled you in what you could do, Mal. The decision is yours."

"Yeah, well, I've never been good at those." Then Mal lowered his head, that cloud of menace returning.

## OF ANGELS FALLEN

He stared down at the knife. "You could have saved her, Jerry. You could have *decided* to do the right thing and saved my mother. But you're a pussy, Jerry."

"I have my instructions, Mal. My job here is to—"

White saw it coming at him, a flash of white and gold hurtling toward his chest. He felt it hit and the pain exploded through his body as if every single nerve had ruptured. His scream was deafening, shaking the very foundation of the building. He looked down and saw the hilt sticking out from the center of his chest. The pain crippling. White fell to his knees, tears streaming down his cheeks. He looked up at Mal as he approached. "Why?" was the only word he could manage.

Mal stepped up close to White and leaned down to whisper in his ear. "Because I don't like being played and I don't like *pussies*." And with that Mal grasped the hilt of the blade and pulled. And as the last sliver of the blade left White's body, Mal could feel all the angel's energy follow the blade out. The room began to tremble. The windows bowed in and White let out another earth-shattering cry. And suddenly Mal found himself at ground zero as White's body exploded with the energy of a thousand suns.

When the sound finally abated, Mal found himself on his knees in the middle of what used to be the top floor of Jericho White's office building. He was trembling, but not with fear, with power. The Blade of

Undoing was still clutched in his hand and he could feel its vibration coursing through his body. It sang to him.

He stood and let the power overtake his battered body and let loose a roar loud enough for the entire city to hear.

He turned to leave, his decision made. He needed to pay an old friend a visit and thank him for all the wonderful gifts he had given him. Then Gregory would feel the sting of *undoing*. And after that Mal would seek out every last angel and undo them in turn.

Gregory was right about one thing. Mal would open the gates of Heaven, but there would be no parade of forgotten angels trailing him through. For when Mal was done slaughtering the angels here on earth he was going for the ones in Heaven. *Oh yeah*, Mal thought, *Heaven will be mine*. Because when he finished with those sons-of-bitches, he was going after God. And that motherfucker was gonna pay.

Travis watched as the claw emerged from the wall of smoke before him. The skin was green, or red, or reddish green, he couldn't tell. Travis shrugged—it was *some* color—who cares? His nose twitched as a horrid stench invaded it, reaching deep into his body, wrapping around his brain, snaking down into his stomach, through to his lower guts and out his asshole with a meaty, slightly wet-sounding and totally violent fart. Travis blushed.

A low rumbling sound arose from the wall of smoke. "Nice one."

All the previous *blush* left Travis' face in a flash, replaced, instead, with a deathly pale white. "Uh-uh," he stammered and took a step back as the claw began fanning the smoke away in a way that Travis found kind of...*girlie*.

Then he heard a heavy blowing sound—like you make when blowing out a candle, only wetter—but not as wet as Travis' earlier fart, of which he was certain there had to be visible evidence marking his shorts—and the wall of smoke began to disappear and the space was soon filled with a creature even Travis wasn't expecting.

Travis stood there, his jaw hanging so low that it was possible he would begin drooling any second. Either that, or he was going to piss himself.

Travis followed the claw up and up. It flowed into an arm as big as Travis' torso. Ridiculously defined muscles were covered with a roadwork of veins and sinew that led to the beast's body which was easily three men wide. Well, at least two big men and maybe one skinny. And on top of the torso sat such an abortion of God's creation Travis didn't know whether to feel pity or scrub pots with the thing's face. Travis' neck began to hurt from looking up at the beast that was easily eight feet tall. He wanted to look away, but he was so entranced—or was it disgusted—that he just couldn't. And Travis continued staring even as the massive claw—the palm of which was bigger than Travis' head—reached out toward him. He didn't even notice as the claw moved close, closer, so close to Travis' face. The talons curled slightly in. And the thumb and middle finger came together and then…

…*thwick*…

…flicked Travis square in the forehead.

"Snap out of it, Chico," the booming voice said flatly. "I know, I know, I'm so fucking gorgeous you just can't stop staring, right?"

"Uh-uh," Travis said, continuing his new adventures in eloquence.

The beast put both arms out, palms facing Travis. "Wait, wait!" he said, motioning with his hands in a, once-again, girlie way. "You think this is good? You need to see the backside." And with that the beast jumped up, spun around in the air, landing with a resounding *thud* and cocked his ass out for Travis to see, which wasn't hard since the creature, being eight feet tall…well…his ass was kind of right in Travis' line of sight.

"Take a look at that, my man. Tell me that isn't the sweetest ass you've ever seen on this plane or any other."

Travis took a small step back, thought about it, and took a *big* step even further back, gave a quick nod and agreed. "Um, yeah. It's a very…nice ass."

The beast wiggled his glorious ass at Travis. "Damn straight, Chico. This thing is a bitch magnet." Then he wagged it one more time, slapped it hard on the right cheek, jumped up, spun around again, and landed facing Travis, his huge, red, cat eyes focusing on the trembling little shit before him.

"Alright, Chico. What the hell do you want?"

The question snapped Travis out of his stupor and he immediately launched into his well-practiced speech: "For years I have sought the means to summon you, oh Lord. I have scoured the globe searching for the spell

# DADDY DEMON'S DAY OUT

that would bring you to me and deliver me that which my heart so desires." Travis emphasized parts of his speech with hand gestures that the beast deemed forced and staged. "From the great plains of Africa, to caves buried deep in the South American jungles and in the highest mountains of Asia, I have…"

"Wait a sec…"

"…killed and destroyed countless in the search for…"

"Hold on now…"

"…the one thing that would…"

"SHUT THE FUCK UP!"

One thing a person should always know when dealing with an eight-foot-tall demon, when they tell you to "SHUT THE FUCK UP!" you…shut the fuck up. So that's what Travis did.

"Look at me, Chico." The beast leaned down so he was eye to eye with Travis. "Do I fucking look like I care what you did to summon me? Huh, *do I?*"

Travis was as surprised by the question as he was by the fresh, minty breath of the beast. He kind of expected: dead, rotten meat, sulfur, a huge unwashed ass. Still, Travis was told he would have to show his dedication to the demon. Show the trials and difficulties he went through to acquire the spell and the implements needed to summon the beast. "Well, I was told I had to…"

"Yeah, yeah." The beast stood back up to full height, rolling his eyes. "I know, you were told I need to know just how much you went through to call me, blah, fucking blah."

"But…" Travis feebly tried to interject.

"See, Chico, you ain't the first to call me and it's always the same old story and I don't really fucking care anymore. Besides, all you had to do was go to a machine at a small grocery store on 5th and 26th and the spell is in one of those temporary tattoo dispensers, you dumbass." The beast shook his head in disgust at Travis. "So tell me what you want and we can get this shit over with."

Travis was a little dumbfounded. He knew what he wanted, but *that* came at the end of his speech. And now he scrambled to run through his entire diatribe in his mind. *What did I want?* he thought. *Fuck!* "Well…"

But before he could get anything else out, the giant claw quickly dropped and clamped to his head. Travis soon found himself about two feet off the ground looking directly into the demon's face, and once again, smelling his lovely, minty breath.

"And let me say this up front, Chico. It had better be fucking good or I'm gonna swallow you whole and let you pass through my digestive system alive. And believe me, there are nasty-ass things down there." Travis' eyes were wide with fear and he felt a nice warmth spread down his left leg. "Ever heard of a bunklewart?" Travis tried to shake his head, but since it was held firmly in place by the beast's grip, he just sort of shook in the air like a ragdoll. "Nasty little bugger. Ate it on a dare a couple millennia ago. Little bastard is still down there. Likes to poke his head out every now and then when I take a dump. Never been able to get him out, though. You *do not* want to meet him in a dark place. And trust me, Chico, it's damn dark all up in my hole. Know what I mean?"

Again Travis tried to nod, only hurting his neck in the process. Then the beast let go and Travis fell in a heap on the floor. He quickly gathered his legs under him and stood, brushing himself off.

"You can't harm me. You serve me," Travis said only half-believing what he was saying.

"Wanna try that one out?" The demon's eyes glowed as the corners of his deformed mouth turned upward.

The grin that crossed the beast's face told Travis that he had received some even more bad information. *Shit!* he thought. "But I thought if I called you to me you would have to do what I commanded."

The beast huffed, disgusted. "I don't have to do shit for you, my man. I *can* do something for you as a reward for bringing me up out of The Pit, but I don't *have* to."

Travis looked around confused and eventually glanced at the ground at the large circle he had put there to contain the demon. He felt a glimmer of hope. He spent years killing virgins, cremating them and gathering their ashes to form the circle. He waved his hand toward the ring of gray dust. "The Circle of

Confinement bids you stay where you were summoned. You cannot..."

But before he could finish the beast dropped to his knees, leaned down and stuck his right nostril—which was about ten times the size of his left—into the circle of virgin ashes. He put all his weight on one knee, cocked his glorious ass in the air and spun himself around a full 360 degrees. It happened in a flash and when he was finished, the entire ring of ash was gone, inhaled deeply into the beast's cavernous nostril.

"Your 'Circle of Confinement' blows, Chico." And he jumped up, leaned into Travis and said softly while tapping his ash-covered nostril, "Between me and you...some of them weren't virgins."

Travis was stunned...all that work.

"But I wouldn't worry about it," consoled the demon, "pretty much impossible to find a hundred virgins these days. Shit, even back in the day it was hard to find a good crop of virgins." The demon struck a demure pose and his voice changed to that of a young woman, "Why I assure you, sir, my yummy bits remain as kosher as the day I was born." Then he dropped the woman act. "Meanwhile, she just got done spreading her *virginal* herpes to the entire infield of the 1919 Brooklyn Dodgers." Then he shook his head sadly. "Women, huh?"

Travis stepped backwards, and kept moving until the back of his legs met the seat of a chair and he collapsed into its worn leather. All that he worked for, everything he had planned for so long…all for nothing. He was devastated.

The beast, seeing Travis' hound dog expression, slowly approached him. He crouched down, tilted his head and gave Travis a look of concern. Or what he thought was one. His gnarled and lumpy face was hard to read.

"Look… Uh, what's your name, Chico?"

Travis muttered something.

"What? Speak up, boy."

"Travis. I said my name is Travis."

"Well, Travis, what say you and I hit the town? See some sights, maybe a little rape, slaughter some innocents, get a cheese steak…? But between you and me, I say we get the cheese steak first. I'm freakin' hungry. Whadda'ya say?"

Travis looked up into the demon's grotesque face. "Do I have a choice?" he asked with a little more than a hint of bitterness in his voice.

The demon moved in close, practically touching Travis' nose with his own. Or it might have been his cheek or lip—who knows—it all blended together into a lumpy mess. Kind of like head cheese, without the gelatinous goo to give it some shape. "Check your tone with me, little man. I'm pretty easy going, but don't think for a minute I won't snap your neck," he threatened. But then he pulled back and mussed up Travis' hair. "And besides, play along and we'll see what we can do about these *desires* of yours."

Travis was stunned. "You mean you still might grant me…"

"Ah, ah, ah… We'll see. Depends on how I feel after we go apeshit out on the town. We have fun, I'll listen to what you want. But not until then. Deal?"

Travis' spirits soared. Finally, some hope. "Okay. Whatever you want to do." He stood, smoothing his clothes. "Where to first?"

The demon stood to full height, put his claw to his chin and adopted a look of serious pondering. "Hmmm. You know what… I would kill for a frappuccino. Is there a Starbucks around?"

Travis let out an amused huff. "Isn't there always?"

The demon let loose a tremendous laugh that shook the floor. "True dat, my man. True dat." Then he slapped Travis on the back, almost knocking him to his knees. "Lead on, chico, lead on. But you might wanna change your pants…you pissed yourself."

Travis blushed with embarrassment.

«« — »»

Travis had seen some pretty sick shit. A lot of it had even been at his hands. But right now, the display in front of him was rivaling even the sickest stuff he had done.

## DADDY DEMON'S DAY OUT

The beast sat in front of Travis consuming his fifteenth cheese steak. But Travis wasn't sure if even one complete sandwich had made it into that atrocious mouth. The remnants of the other fourteen lay strewn in a good three-foot circle around their table. It was a blast zone of soggy bread, slimy, grilled onions and peppers mixed with some low-grade meat.

Dewanal—and you could bet he did too—chomped with glee upon his sandwich. His face, hands and chest glistened with grease. "Holy fucking shit, Travis, it's like I cum with every bite," he said, spewing bits of food all over himself, *and* Travis, *and* the window, *and* the floor, *and* a baby and her horrified parents two tables away who suddenly decided they had someplace better to be.

Travis thought Dew's—that's what he was told to call the demon—show earlier at a Starbuck's was bad enough. The demon had consumed enough lattes, frappuccinos, and espressos to tweak out a small army. Travis had been fine with his non-fat, half-decaf, half soy, mochacino, no whip. Tall. Dew called him a fag while spewing foam from his deformed mouth. Now this…

"Bitch, you need to eat one of these things. I mean seriously, it's better than sex." The demon paused, "Well…most sex." Then he roared with laughter, giving the floor another coat of chewed up food.

«« — »»

"So how come I can't see what everyone else sees?" Travis asked, hoping Dew would let him see the human façade that everyone else saw instead of the mess he had to look at.

"Aw, what'sa matta, baby. You don't find me pretty anymore?" Then Dew let out an anguished sob and started huffing as if caught up in a deep crying fit. "You used…to think I-I-I…was sexy."

Travis sat there, jaw hanging open.

"Remember when you used to call me your little pretty pony and ride me all night long? Huh, do you?" cried Dew.

The people in the restaurant who toughed it out during the feeding frenzy stared at the two of them. Everyone likes a free display of drama.

"You were the one who wanted kids, not me. You're the one who said you'd pull out. You bastard!" Dew shouted, standing and slamming the table with his palm. "You're the one that did this to me. You ruined me and now you don't want to fuck me anymore. Well, fuck you, Mr. Man."

Travis shot uneasy looks at those around him. Even people on the street were looking in the window.

Dew's theatrics were in full-gear. Tears running down his face, wheezing, trying to catch his breath between sobs. "Well, you just go off to your fucking whore. We're through and I'm taking you for everything, you cheating bastard." Dew stood there panting for a second or two, then stormed out, leaving Travis with all eyes focused on him.

Travis slowly stood up and tried to keep his composure while getting the hell out there as fast as he could. He smoothed his jacket, as was his habit, slid the chair through the grease-covered floor into place under the table, gave a slight nod to everyone watching, turned and casually walked out the door.

He caught up with Dew about a block away. "So I take it everyone sees you as a woman?"

"I thought it would be fun," Dew said somewhat distracted, as if looking for something.

"Nice."

Dew shrugged. "Strippers."

"What?"

"Strippers, whores, women. Need some titty in my face. Need to put my log in the fire."

Travis just stared at Dew, stunned by his *eloquence*. "Wow," was all he could say for a minute.

"What? When was the last time you went all raw dog on a bitch?"

Travis stood silent.

"Exactly," Dew said slapping Travis on the back. "We need pussy."

Travis started to protest, then stopped, thought a

minute. He could stand to get laid. It *had* been a long time. When he did have sex it was usually part of some rite or ritual and always ended in him covered in blood and shit. Would be nice to just find a hot whore and just have her fuck his brains out.

"Okay, we *need* pussy. Only problem is, there are no strip clubs or hookers around here that I know of. Kind of a conservative town."

Dew started to say something, stopped before any words came out, sniffed the air. "Vegas."

"What?"

"Vegas. We need to go to Vegas."

"It's like 2000 miles away. How the hell are we going to get to there?"

Dew smiled—maybe, who knew with that face—and pulled Travis close. "Hang on, baby. Daddy's just bought us a ticket on the Cooter Caboose."

Dew raised his arm high in the air and started swirling it around. Travis could feel a shower of energy fall down around them. He had a sudden feeling of complete claustrophobia. The air was forced from his lungs as the energy wrapped itself around him, squeezing tighter and tighter.

He saw it coming like a wall barreling toward his face—darkness—pure, pitch black, scary-as-hell darkness. Then it hit him full-on and Travis fell hard and fast into its cold embrace.

# DADDY DEMON'S DAY OUT

«« — »»

*Knock, knock, knock.*

Travis shot bolt upright in his bed. "What the hell?" he said, panting. He shook his head trying to get the images from a nightmare out of his head. He was wrapped in his sheets, or more like glued to them. His entire body was covered in sweat. He started to struggle with the soaking wet sheets and quickly gave up and just sat in the middle of his bed, dazed and confused.

Travis never had nightmares—*never*—until just now and man was it a doozie. He wasn't even sure what had happened in the dream. Just chaos, blood and screaming. And in the middle his wife… She was…that guy… *What the fuck?* was all Travis could think.

*Knock, knock, knock.*

"Shit," Travis said, realizing someone was at the door. He tried to get up and—*thud*—quickly found himself face down on the floor, the sheets firmly wrapped around his legs. "God *damn* it!"

*Knock, knock, knock.*

"Hold on," Travis yelled. He rolled onto his back and began furiously kicking his legs to loosen the sheets.

*Knock, knock, knock.*

"I'm coming. One second. Christ!" A couple of more kicks and Travis was finally free. He pushed himself up and spun around trying to get his bearings. He saw his robe, grabbed it, and headed toward the door while pulling it on.

*Knock, knock, knock.*

"Keep it in your pants! I'm coming."

*Knock, knock, knock.*

Travis was getting pissed. He reached the front door, grabbed the handle, turned it and yanked the door open hard. "Son of a bi—"

Travis cut himself off when he saw the two uniformed men standing in front of him. The dour looks on their faces told him something was wrong—*very* wrong.

"Mr. Burnsfield?" asked the one on the right.

"Uh, yeah."

"Mr. Travis Burnsfield?"

"Uh-huh."

The two officers stood there giving Travis an up and down with their eyes. Then they gave each other a quick look as if deciding to continue. "May we come in, sir?" asked the same officer.

"Umm, well... Ah," Travis realized he was sounding like a babbling idiot, but he was a little stunned to see two cops at his doorstep. He took a second and pulled it together. "Sure. Please," he said and stood to the side to let the officers in.

He led them to the living room and offered them a seat. Neither took one. Instead: "I think it best if you sat down, Mr. Burnsfield."

*Shit,* Travis thought. *This isn't good.* So he sat. He

didn't do it because they told him he should. He sat because he knew what they were going to say. *Oh, God, he thought, I know what they're going to say.*

The same officer began talking again. "Mr. Burnsfield, your wife…"

*No, not Sally…*

"Mrs. Sally Burnsfield…"

*Oh, God…*

"Well, we're very sorry, Mr. Burnsfield, but there was an incident at the school today."

*An incident?*

"At approximately 11:20 this morning a man entered Jefferson Elementary. He worked his way to the classroom of your wife." The officer paused. He was trying to stay calm and be cool and distant, but Travis could tell he was having a hard time. The other officer just looked at a spot somewhere above Travis' head, chewing his bottom lip.

"And after entering your wife's classroom the man pulled a knife and well…" It was as if he suddenly decided that the details weren't all that crucial right now. "Your wife was rushed to the hospital, but was pronounced dead on arrival."

The other officer finally lowered his eyes and looked right at Travis who had looked to him as though trying to ask if this was a joke. Finally the other officer spoke, "We're very, very sorry, Mr. Burnsfield."

"Yes," said the first one. "Rest assured we have

every officer available looking for this man. And I promise you—"

The words just filled the space between Travis and the officers. All Travis could hear was a loud *hum* as the officers babbled on—a *hum*, a *buzz*, then just static. And then he saw it coming—a wall of darkness barreling toward his face—pure, pitch-black, scary-as-hell darkness. Then it hit him full-on and Travis fell hard and fast into its cold embrace.

«« — »»

"Hey, T-man."

Travis felt himself being shook. "Sally?" he croaked groggily.

"What? No, man. Come on. Snap out of it. We're here."

Travis felt a hand gripping his shoulder, shaking him some more. "Here? What?" Travis said trying to get his head to stop spinning.

A loud, boisterous voice answered him back, "Vegas, baby. *VEGAS!*"

Travis was finally recovering from the effects of the trip. He looked up and immediately closed his eyes to the assault of light from a million flashing, colored light bulbs. "Fuck!"

Dew looked down at Travis and laughed. "Trip a little rough on ya, buddy? Here…" And Dew touched Travis' forehead very delicately and suddenly Travis felt fine.

# DADDY DEMON'S DAY OUT

"Damn. Thanks."

"Uh-huh," said Dew distractedly. It was obvious his mind had already moved on to better things. "You know what?"

"Uh... Let me guess... Pussy," Travis said knowingly.

"Ab-so-fucking-lutely. Daddy's dip stick needs to check some bitch's fluid. Know what I mean?"

"Well, although masterfully subtle, I think I get your innuendo."

Dew laughed, "I like you, T-man." Then he raised his arm and Travis braced himself for a hard slap on the back. But just before the hand reached him, Dew yelled, "Psyche," and mussed up Travis' hair instead. "Let's roll."

And they were moving. Travis had to laugh; here he was, walking down the Vegas strip next to a demon he had just summoned a couple of hours ago. *This is like some sort of fucked up Harold and Maude shit,* he thought. He looked up at the abomination next to him and wondered what others were seeing. "What are you now?"

"Huh?"

"What are people seeing you as? Still a woman?"

"Hell, yeah. And you wouldn't believe the rack I got. And of course my ass is perfect. I'm so hot, I'd fuck me—" Dew looked down at Travis, eyes wide. "—twice."

"So where are we going?"

"Little place hidden off one of the side streets. Anything goes there. Private parties for special customers."

"And I take it you've been there before?"

"Shit yeah. Lots. Been around a long time. Kind of a traveling sex depot. Just so happens you summoned me at the right time, T-man. Cuz it being here in Vegas makes it even more special."

"Why?"

"'Cuz after we get done we can go gamble. And, baby, Daddy feels lucky tonight."

Travis had to walk fast to keep up with the lumbering demon. They reached the end of the Strip and Dew kept going. The buildings got sparser and dirtier. The lights began to fade off into the distance. Dew made a turn here, a turn there and Travis realized he had no idea where they were or how to get back to the main street. He worried for a second before remembering he was with a fucking demon. Anyone jumped them, they were in for a big surprise.

"So where is this place?"

Dew stopped so abruptly Travis actually walked past him before realizing it.

"We're here, baby."

Travis looked around confused. All he could see were old warehouses. "I don't see anything."

Dew grabbed Travis by his head and turned it. "There," he said flatly.

Travis saw him—a man in the distance, standing in front of a big metal door. "Oh. Kind of low-key, huh?"

"Wait until you get inside. It's anything but."

# DADDY DEMON'S DAY OUT

"Oh yeah?"

"T-man, get ready to experience every carnal pleasure you've ever imagined. 'Cuz you're about to enter a myth, a legend."

"Big build up."

"You got that right. I already got a little drip on my tip just thinking about what's going on in there." Dew looked down at Travis. "You ready, T-man?"

Travis was concerned. If a demon was excited about the shit going in there it *must* be fucked up. But again, he had to admit, he was curious now. "Uh, sure." And that slap on the back he expected earlier finally landed, propelling him forward unexpectedly.

"HA! I like you, T-man." Dew clapped his hands and rubbed them together. "Now… Let's go fuck shit up."

«« — »»

The doorman stood silent as Dew approached. The guy was pretty much a flesh mountain—tall and wide and bald. If Travis hadn't been hanging out with Dew all night he might have been even more impressive, but he was dwarfed by the demon. Still, something told Travis that even a demon would be in for some serious shit if he were to piss this guy off. Something about him screamed one bad-ass-mother-fucker. He offered the demon a slight nod. Dew returned the nod but didn't say anything.

In a blink a slim Asian man slipped from the shadows next to the giant, startling Travis. Dressed completely in black, the man melded with the night. Travis had a hard time seeing him clearly until he stepped into the light hanging over the door. "Dew."

"Horatio...my...man," Dew said extending his hand.

"Been awhile, my demon friend."

"Too long," Dew agreed, still holding his hand out. Finally Horatio reached out toward Dew, but didn't shake his hand. Horatio's fingers closed tight around Dew's wrist, but they didn't stay there. They grew longer, snaking up and around Dew's forearm, constricting tighter and tighter. Then with his other hand, Horatio placed his index finger lightly on Dew's hand. The sickly sweet smell of burning flesh crept into Travis' nose as smoke curled up from Dew's hand.

Horatio looked at Dew with tired, lazy eyes. "About fifty years, or so."

Dew nodded, "Yeah."

"Your mark was almost gone."

Dew laughed looking down as Horatio's fingers slowly retracted back into his hand. "Well, shit, man, you know I'd be here every night if I could. But I have to wait 'til I'm called."

Horatio shot Dew a quick grin before flicking his head in Travis' direction. "This the one who called you?"

Dew grabbed Travis by the neck, picked him up and placed him in front of Horatio. "Yep, *this* is T-man."

Horatio considered Travis for a few moments, then gave a slight courteous nod. "Will you be joining us tonight."

"Ummm…"

"Hell, yeah, he'll be joining you tonight," Dew interrupted. "Travis here needs his pipes cleaned big time. Don'cha, T-man?"

"Apparently I need to get laid or something," Travis said nervously.

"Meager desires for our establishment, but I suppose we can provide you with whatever you'd like." Horatio looked Travis in the eyes. "Hand please."

Travis hesitated.

"Come on, buddy. Give Horatio your hand so you can get your mark. It only stings a little."

"I really don't want to be scarred," Travis said, pointing to Dew's arm.

"What scar?" Dew said holding his arm for Travis to see. And it was true, there was no burnt skin, no harsh scar. Travis had to look closely to see the faint image of a bone. But as he continued to stare, the image faded away. "But I saw him burning you. I smelled your flesh…"

"No visible mark. Now stop being a pussy and give him your hand so we can get this party started."

Travis slowly brought his hand up and, like a cobra

striking, Horatio grabbed it—and before Travis could react—the snake fingers had traveled halfway up his forearm. He could feel heat on his skin.

"Man up, Travis," Dew said, watching intently.

His flesh was burning. He could feel the fire penetrating deep down under the skin, making its way to the bone. He could smell his flesh as it sizzled under the doorman's vise-like grip. Travis thought his teeth would break as the pain increased and he clenched his jaw, struggling to contain a scream. Then...

...it was over. Just like that.

"See, it only stings for a second," Dew said patting Travis on the back.

"Stings?" Travis said irritably.

"Well, you know..." Dew shrugged.

Travis was rubbing his arm furiously. There was no mark, no burn, but he could still feel something there.

"Welcome to Painfreak, Mr. Burnsfield," said Horatio.

"H-how did you know..."

"Horatio knows everyone. Don't you, man?"

"It is my job. I wish you the best in there, gentlemen. May all your desires be satiated." Then he stepped sideways and was gone. Lost in the shadows once more.

"Hell, yeah!" Dew bellowed, turning to the opening door. "Satiate the fuck out of me, brother." Dew grabbed Travis by the neck again and shoved him toward the dark passageway. "Let's do this."

# DADDY DEMON'S DAY OUT

Travis felt himself being propelled into the darkness. And it was cold, so god damn…

«« — »»

…cold.

Travis stood shivering in a waiting room devoid of…anything. The walls were pale grey, surrounding a pale green floor, topped by an even paler grey ceiling and all lit in soul-draining electric brilliance. Institutional was all Travis could think. Sucked dry of all life, all warmth. The perfect setting for what lay beyond its doors. Doors that Travis had been staring at for five minutes.

*Crash!*

Travis jumped as the doors exploded into the room, and through them came a man just as devoid of any detail or life as the room he entered. "Oh… Mr. Burnsfield. Sorry. Didn't mean to startle you."

*Yes you did, you prick,* Travis thought, trying to get his heart back to a non-heart-attack-inducing rate.

"We're ready for you whenever you are, sir," said the grey little man, flatly.

Travis wanted to punch the little shit in the face for his lack of caring. But then he figured the guy had probably done this a hundred times, likely even more. You probably had to be a cold-ass bastard to deal with what he did every day. So Travis gave an internal shrug and walked toward the man who was holding open one of the swinging doors.

The police told Travis he didn't need to identify the body. They knew who she was. But Travis had insisted. He wanted to see his wife… Well, not *wanted* to. He *had* to. He had to see her as she was before the morticians got a hold of her and painted her up like a fucking doll for the public to see before hiding her away in the ground to become a distant memory to those who knew her: *Hey, remember that woman we worked with who got killed back in '64? Yeah, what was her name?*

*Her name was Sally*, Travis thought, *and she was my wife and I loved her more than life itself.*

Travis found himself standing in front of a gurney in another room even colder and more lifeless than the last. The coroner moved around to the other side of the gurney from Travis. "Are you ready?"

The question bounced around inside Travis' head. *No. No, I'm not ready,* he thought. Then he shot the man a quick nod while the rest of his body remained board stiff.

The man grabbed the end of the sheet, lifted it slightly and then slowly pulled it back. He stopped just below the shoulders and set the sheet down gently. Travis saw the man's hands move away, but he continued staring at the edge of the sheet so white against his wife's grey flesh. Travis slowly moved his eyes down his wife's body, seeing a slight rise where her breasts pressed up from under the sheet. Then back down briefly until the sheet rose again above the little pooch of belly. Sally had complained about it all the time. But Travis had always assured her she was perfect. He loved spooning her after sex, wrapping his arm around her and placing his open hand atop her stomach. She may have hated her belly, but she loved it when Travis caressed it. She would place her hand on top of his and press down while snuggling deeper into his embrace. And they would fall asleep like that, nestled into each other…perfection.

Travis could feel the tears building in his eyes. His chest was tightening. That hum of static growing louder. Then—

"…so we didn't really need to do much except for clean up the wound."

Travis snapped out of his memory, looking quickly at the coroner. "What?"

The coroner remained cool and repeated himself flatly. "I was saying that because we know how it happened we didn't really need to do anything invasive in our examination. We just had to sew up the wound and prepare the body…er…your wife… for the mortician."

Then he pointed down at the body and Travis followed the finger down, down, down. And there it was, what he came to see—what he *had* to see—a dark line of split flesh slicing through his wife's neck from ear to ear. It was a brutal slap in Travis' face. He had to tell himself to breathe. This was it. This was the image that would fuel his quest for vengeance for decades: Sally, his one and only *true* love, laid out on a cold metal table. Covered in a cold white sheet, surrounded by cold walls. All her life, all her warmth, her love…gone, stolen in one quick slash across her perfect little throat by some unknown bastard.

Travis stared at the harshly-stitched wound, his tears of grief replaced by tears of rage and hatred.

The coroner's voice snapped Travis out of his daze. "Not sure why you wanted to see her this way, but I hope you got what you came for, whatever it is."

Travis looked the grey little man straight in the eyes. "I had to see for myself what he did to her. I had to know exactly what it is that I need to do to this fucker when I finally catch him," Travis said, his voice as cold and bleak as everything around him.

The man began to say something, then stopped himself, and instead gave Travis an understanding nod as if this weren't the first time he heard someone say something like that. Then he grabbed the edge of the sheet and pulled it up.

«« — »»

"Dude! Seriously, what the fuck?"

"Huh?" Travis snapped out of his memory and was shaking. Dew had his giant claw on Travis' shoulder and was giving him a good jostling.

"Where the fuck do you keep going, my man?" Dew asked still shaking Travis.

## DADDY DEMON'S DAY OUT

"Please stop shaking me."

"Oh, sorry." Dew stopped. "But seriously, you having seizures or something?"

"Don't worry about it," Travis said absently.

Dew shrugged. "Whatever, man." He tried to seem cavalier about it but Travis detected a slight hint of concern in the demon's voice. He didn't know if this was a good or bad thing.

As Travis gathered himself he started looking around and found he was standing in the middle of a bloodbath. Or at least it seemed that way as everything around him was awash in a deep, bloody red. From floor to ceiling, everything…red. It made the narrow tunnel they were in even more claustrophobic.

"Like stepping into a vein. Ain't it?" Dew said.

"Kind of—" But Travis realized Dew had kept moving and was almost out of sight. He hurried to catch up, not wanting to be left alone.

Travis started to turn to catch up with Dew. He came around a slight bend to the left and barreled through a velvet curtain. The first thing that hit him was an assault of bass that threatened to burst his eardrums. The next thing to hit him was Dew's back. It was like hitting a brick wall. Travis staggered back, dazed.

"Easy, boy." And Dew took a step to the side. "We're in…" And he held up his massive arms to the air and spun around. "This is gonna kick so much ass!"

No one seemed to notice the giant demon bellowing

in the middle of the room. The room looked how you would expect a club in an old abandoned warehouse to look: dim, bleak, minimal. The low light hid the dirt and age. Long, plush couches lined the walls, while round sofas dotted the floor in little islands of comfort. All were littered with a human menagerie. Travis had kind of expected to see nothing but Goths in here. He had been to many clubs like this over the years looking for willing souls to participate in his little rituals. But Painfreak was different. There were Goths, sure, but the crowd was more than just that. The only word that seemed fitting to Travis was…normal. Most of the people here looked *normal*. No leather, vinyl, piercings, tattoos or bondage gear. Just normal people dancing, making out…fucking.

Travis was unimpressed. And Dew, as he always seemed to know what Travis was thinking, said, "Don't be disappointed yet. This is just the warm-up area. Let's get some drinks."

Travis shrugged and said, "Alright."

The bar was packed, but a nice wide opening seemed to miraculously appear as Dew approached. And just as he reached the bar, the bartender slid gracefully in front of the demon. Her eyes were a brilliant emerald green and lit up like neon beneath severe black bangs even Bettie Page would envy. Her hair cut off just as severely at her creamy white shoulders. Travis let his eyes wander down the bartender's figure as far as the bar would let him. From what he could tell, she was perfection in female form. And as she parted her dark red lips, Travis waited to hear what the voice of an angel sounded like.

"S'up, Dew, ya fuck?"

Turns out the "voice of an angel" sounded like a 50-year-old trucker from the Bronx named Sal. And apparently, Sal had been smoking since he was in the womb.

Dew turned and looked at Travis who stood there, jaw to the ground, slobbering. You would have thought it was the funniest thing Dew had ever seen as he let loose a belly laugh that rivaled the bass pumping throughout the air. Travis tried to gather himself up as he realized everyone was looking at him now.

Dew slapped his hand on the bar laughing so hard he could barely catch his breath. He eventually pulled it together, "Travis, this here is Bobby. And don't let those eyes and that body fool ya. Bobby's packing enough meat to put even *me* to shame."

Bobby gave Travis a smile that would make any man hand over his wallet, car keys and stock options in a second and followed it up with a neon green wink. Travis almost swooned. Then the voice: "What's da fuck ya doin' with dis shitbag? He ain't nuthin' but trouble...with a capital FUCK YOU!" Then Bobby and Dew exploded with laughter again as the gap at the bar widened a little more.

"Bobby! Set us up with some Mind-Fucks. Travis and I are gonna get tore up and then *tear up* some serious dick warmers."

Bobby snorted. "You'se sure gots a way wit da words, Dew." Then to Travis, "Dis fuck's a real charmer, ain't he?" Then Bobby didn't walk away so much as disappear, only to return in a second with two giant glasses, filled with a purple liquid that Travis could have sworn screamed when Bobby set them on the bar. When Travis blinked, Bobby was at the other end of the bar. Dew crammed one of the drinks into Travis' hand.

"A toast to…"

"…pussy?" Travis said, seeing where this was going.

"TO PUSSY!" Dew yelled. And the rest of the bar joined him, everyone screaming back: "TO PUSSY!"

Travis took a big swig of his Mind-Fuck and…

When Travis came to he found he was staring himself in the face. He quickly looked around only to discover he was standing in the middle of a large room. The relentless bass pounded in the distance. Travis could feel sweat sliding down his back and finding its way into his ass crack. *God it's hot in here,* he thought. His eyes tracked around the room until he saw himself again. He jumped a little, then felt foolish as he realized he was staring into an enormous mirror. "Shit," he said softly, lowering his head shakily. If he had been more observant, Travis would have noticed his reflection *not* do the same.

## DADDY DEMON'S DAY OUT

Travis raised his head again and stared at himself. He was old. But he didn't look as old as he actually was. No, years of dark magic and rituals to extend his life so he could see his plan to the end had hidden his true age. But still, he almost didn't recognize the man in the mirror anymore. Oh, it was him, he knew that, but even with the magic, the years of darkness had had its affect on him. Where once Travis stood well over six feet tall and straight as an arrow, his shoulders now slumped making him look smaller, turtle-like. His eyes sat behind smudged, thick glasses, making them look freakishly large. His bald head was peppered with dark brown spots, and his skin shone white in the dark room as though being lit from inside his body. "I am one pale-ass motherfucker," he said to his image.

"You got that right, brother," agreed his image.

Travis jumped back as if shot.

"And you peed yourself," said his reflec…well it wasn't really his reflection was it—definitely more his image—it didn't mimic Travis' actions at all. In fact, Travis felt hot piss streaming down his leg, but didn't see his image in the mirror doing the same.

Travis stumbled back a couple of steps and quickly found himself on his ass. The fall stunned him as he looked to find out what he had fallen over. He began immediately backpedaling when he saw the young girl painted with the whitish-blue of death at his feet.

Travis' image raised an eyebrow. "Nice work, my man."

"I d-d-didn't…"

The image, grinning and eyes wide, nodded its head. "Oh yeah, you d-d-did."

Travis looked at the girl's body. The first thing he thought was, *no blood*. He followed the curvy contours of her shapely body up, up and up until he saw the necklace of hideous black and blue bruises she wore.

"You sure showed that bitch, huh, buddy?"

"Shut the fuck up," Travis retorted shakily.

Travis' image adopted a confused expression. "You've killed before. I know," he said with a slight grin while tapping his finger against his forehead. Then he shrugged: "What's another dirty whore, right?"

Travis pushed himself up onto his knees. "I said, shut the fuck up!" His voice laced with venom.

The image held up his hands in defeat and took a step back into the darkness of the mirror becoming slightly smaller. "Okay, okay. Easy, buddy. Who am I to say what happened? I mean, after all, I was just there."

The image took a step forward and leaned down a little and looked at Travis sideways. "Wanna see?" He moved off to the side and disappeared from the mirror, all except his hand, which gave a sweeping motion as an usher directing someone to their seat. Then the hand swept itself right out of the scene and all that was left was what Travis guessed was the same room he was currently in. Only there was a lot more light and a lot less death.

## DADDY DEMON'S DAY OUT

Travis sat on the edge of a bed, his head lolling to one side, the effects of the Mindfuck evident on his face by a stupid, wide-ass grin of drunkenness. The door to the room opened and the girl, who was currently dead in front of Travis, walked in. She was dressed in a typical fetish schoolgirl outfit. Travis saw his face appear from the edge of the mirror and toss him a wink. "Fucking love the naughty school girl, don't we? Ironic, huh?"

Travis returned the comment with a cold stare.

"Okay, maybe not ironic. Just fucked up." Then the head disappeared again.

Travis watched as the scene unfolded in front of him like low-grade, homemade porn. The girl danced around, asked if she was naughty and if she would be punished. "Oh, you'll be punished," the drunk Travis said. Then the same voice from off screen, "You show that bitch, boy!" Followed by loud laughter.

Travis didn't appreciate commentary from the audience. The laughter faded as drunk Travis ordered the girl to strip. Which she did, like a pro, all the while performing the shy, scared, little girl act. The girl was ordered to the bed. Travis watched himself bind the girl to the wrought iron headboard with straps he hadn't noticed before. None of this really surprised him as he had done this and worse over the years.

Travis watched himself clumsily strip naked and cringed at his white and shriveled body.

His face appeared again. "When this is all over, we

need to do some serious crunches and shit. We look like crap." Then he shrank off to the side again shaking his head in shame.

The scene had continued and Travis saw himself mounting the girl. He pushed her legs up and placed his hands on the back of her knees and pushed them up as far as he could until her knees were pressed tight against her shoulders. She made some pleasure groans, sticking to the script. Travis laid his weight onto the girls legs to hold her in place so he could fumble his half-hard cock into her exposed and wonderfully-shaved pussy. It was a sad sight, like watching a teenage boy try and fuck for the first time.

"Need a little of the magic Blue-V, my man!"

Travis winced, ashamed that he agreed. He watched himself unromantically and mercilessly pound into the hot, little whore. He kind of wished he remembered some of it; but not for long, because the tone of the scene began to change. Travis' thrusts grew harder and more desperate, he laid into the girl, pinning her beneath his body. He may have been old and not what he once was, but he still weighed a lot more than her and it was clear she was trapped. Then the drunk Travis began yelling. He pounded into the girl, lying directly on top of her. She tried to push him off, but with his body he held her fast as he fell onto her again and again. "Fucking bitch! You like that, whore? Fucking take it! I'm gonna fuck ya til you scream, you fucking whore!"

Travis could see the horror on the girl's face as she quickly realized something had gone terribly wrong. She began to scream out for help.

"You want help, cunt?" Travis yelled. Amid his thrusts he managed to slap her hard in the face. "Shut your fucking face!"

Travis sat in stunned silence. He had never done anything like this before in his life. Even in the most twisted orgies and sexual sacrificial rituals he had never behaved like this. It couldn't be him, but there he was. "No…"

His face appeared just enough for him to see his eyes. "Oh, yes…" Then the eyes disappeared.

The scene in front of him was deteriorating exponentially. The girl continued to scream and drunk Travis mocked her and screamed back in her face. "SHUT UP! SHUT UP! SHUT UP! SHUT UP! SHUT UP!" Panic was setting in as the scene grew frantic. The girl squirmed and tried to shake Travis off her, but to no avail. "I warned you, bitch!" And that's when the thrusting stopped and both of Travis' hands came up and wrapped themselves around the girl's neck. "I said…shut…the…fuck…up!" Drunk Travis grunted after every word, the sweat pouring off his face and dripping on to the girl. His hands squeezed harder and the girl squirmed more and more. The bed was a whirlwind of squirming limbs. Travis pressed the girl down into the mattress by her neck, squeezing, squeezing, squeezing until…*snap!* Something in her neck gave way and abruptly her limbs fell to the sweat soaked sheets as Travis collapsed on top of her.

He stayed there panting on top of the girl for a few seconds as he began to cry and tears mixed with his dripping sweat, dropping into the dead girl's hair. Then Travis pushed himself back as the realization of what he had just done hit him like a slap to the face. His face twisted in drunk surprise and then…horror. He fumbled backward getting caught up in the sheets and quickly found himself tumbling out of control off the end of the bed. Travis watched in shock as his drunk self landed head first onto the hardwood floor, his limp body crumbling into a pile at the foot of the bed.

"Annnnd… End scene!" screamed Travis' voice from the darkness. The current state of the room appeared in the mirror again and Travis watched himself appear from the side. He was clapping slowly and loudly. "Not sure what I think of the final scene. The lead actor's performance was flaccid and, although gorgeous and sensual, the actress's performance turned stiff in the end."

Travis gave himself a look that said: *Go fuck yourself.*

"Aw, what's a matter? Afraid you're becoming that which you hunt?"

"I didn't do that," Travis said flatly.

His image shrugged, "Whatever, man. Believe what

# DADDY DEMON'S DAY OUT

you want. You know what you are and what you're capable of. This is nothing." Then the image's eyes widened. "Oh, man! You know what I just thought? What if... Now get this, right. What if...this bitch you just killed has a husband or boyfriend who gets so pissed off that he decides to commit the rest of his life to tracking *her* murderer down. Now *that*...would be fucking irony!"

Travis bolted from the floor and launched himself at the mirror, trying to tackle his image. But all he found was the cold resistance of hard glass. He bounced off.

"Easy, boy!" yelled his image. But he didn't move, knowing full well Travis couldn't get to him. "You're just going to hurt yourself...hurt us."

But Travis ignored the warning and rebounded, firing his fist into his image's face. The glass didn't give, but something in his hand did as it smashed into the glass. He screamed at the pain, at his anger, at himself, "You fuck."

"Christ. Look at you. You think this is what Sally would have wanted? You think she would have wanted you to waste your life on pointless revenge?"

"Shut the fuck up!" Travis screamed, pounding his fists against the unbreakable glass.

"Let's ask her." And Travis' image disappeared and then...there she was, his wife—his beautiful wife. He backed up a couple of steps, stunned.

She looked at him with concern. "Travis, honey. What are you doing?"

Travis slowly reached out to her, his fingers lightly touched the cold, lifeless glass, and he cried. "I'm so…sorry." He dropped to his knees and hung his head in shame, sobbing uncontrollably. "I just wanted…"

"Shhhh, baby," Sally said. "I know, I know. You just wanted to avenge me. That's sweet. Really. But did you for one minute think that because of all this…darkness you've surrounded yourself in would only lead to one place?"

Travis looked up into the heavenly face of his wife and shrunk back in horror as he saw she was completely naked. His image appeared behind her and reached its hands around Sally and began rubbing her up and down. Sally's face became a mask of ecstasy. She moaned as the hands traced the curves on her body, reaching down in between her sex, back up to cup and fondle her breasts. She arched her back and ground her round ass into the image's hard cock. Travis snapped, he screamed and launched himself at the mirror and when he hit it, he kept pushing himself against the cold glass as if he pushed hard enough he could break through the barrier and reach his dead wife. But nothing gave way, and eventually Travis slid down the sweat-streaked glass, screaming and crying, "Stop. Just…stop!" He became lost in his own tears as he continually screamed for the scene in the mirror to stop. But all he heard were moans and laughter. And…

*BANG! BANG! BANG!*

## DADDY DEMON'S DAY OUT

"T-man! You in there?"

Dew's voice was far, far in the distance, lost amid the pounding bass.

"T! Open the fucking door!" *BANG! BANG! BANG!* "Fuck this!"

*BANG! BANG! BANG!*

*CRASH!*

The door behind Travis exploded inward and Dew burst into the room, naked and glistening with sweat, his cock rock hard and leading his way by at least a foot. It bounced ahead of him as he ran toward Travis. "What the fuck is going on? T-man, what's wrong?" Then he stopped and looked in the mirror and saw the scene that dropped Travis to his knees. "Mother fucker!" Dew yelled. His eyes, what could be seen of them, burned red. His entire body seemed to grow as he seethed with anger. "You fucking little prick!" And he reached out toward Travis, whose eyes grew wild with fear at the monstrous demon coming straight for him. But just as he thought Dew's claw would grab his head and squeeze it like a grape, he saw it shoot over and past his head and reach right into the mirror. Travis took this as an opportune moment to back the fuck up and get to his feet.

Dew grunted, "Come here, you little piece of shit!"

Travis watched as his wife disappeared and Dew's claw wrapped itself around his image inside the mirror. Dew clasped Travis' doppelganger by the neck, yanked, and pulled a pale, white and very scared creature out of the mirror with a harsh sucking sound. There was a loud rumbling and then the sound of breaking glass filled the room followed by a deafening shriek and the mirror exploded inward, shards firing deep into a black hole that rapidly grew smaller and smaller until—*POP!*—there was nothing there—nothing but a large and very pissed off demon dangling a creature—that no longer looked like Travis—by the neck.

Dew pulled what looked like a marionette of twigs covered in ashy grey skin close to his face. "Boscoe, I...am...going...to...fucking snap your fucking neck, you fucking fuck!"

The creature's whole body shook with fear, its head the size of a beach ball bobbing atop its popsicle stick neck. "D-D-D-Dew! I'm sorry, man. I didn't know he was with you! I'm sorry! I'm sorry!"

Dew squeezed Boscoe's neck and Travis was amazed it hadn't snapped yet. Despite its enormous head, the creature had a surprisingly small mouth, and two slight slits that indicated where a nose should be if he in fact had one. And absolutely no eyes. Travis was completely creeped out. "What the fuck is that?" he yelled.

Dew gave the little beast a couple more shakes for good measure before turning the stickman to face Travis. "This is a...Boscoe. A low-life piece of shit."

Boscoe brought a bony hand up. It looked made of wires and leather. He gave Travis a quick wave. "Hi," he croaked.

# DADDY DEMON'S DAY OUT

Travis looked at Boscoe. He tried to say something, but nothing came out. Instead his left eye started twitching, and he began to tremble. So he hauled off and punched Boscoe right in his big fucking head.

"Ow, fuck!" Boscoe screamed. "He fucking punched me! You fucking sack of shit, you punched me."

Dew pulled Boscoe to his face again and they looked at each other, fucked-up features to fucked-up features. "And…?" He turned Boscoe back toward Travis. "Hit 'im again, T. Hard!"

And Travis did. Once, twice, three times, and he just kept hitting the little beast. And the more Boscoe screamed the harder he hit him, battering his balloon head mercilessly until a black fluid began leaking from various places on Boscoe. Travis hit again and again until he had no more energy to even swing his arms anymore. So he feebly reached up and flicked Boscoe in his slit of a nose.

"Ow! Fuck!" Boscoe cried, his words bubbly through the black blood leaking from his mouth.

Dew reached down to one of Boscoe's legs, grabbed it in his hand and twisted it until there was an audible crack, followed by a scream that made Travis' asshole quiver. "There, now you won't be going anywhere," said Dew casually. Then he tossed Boscoe into a corner where he landed in a pile of angled limbs and bulbous, bleeding head.

Dew turned to Travis. "You alright, man?"

Travis nodded dully. Then nodding his head toward the moaning pile in the corner, "What the hell is that?"

Dew shook his head and waved his hand as if dismissing Boscoe as inconsequential. "It's a Boscoe." Then he looked at the whimpering creature. "A fucking little parasite."

Between moans Boscoe managed a, "Fuck you too, Dew!"

"I take it you know each other?" asked Travis.

"Oh yeah. He's a fucking bastard. An abomination," said Dew, disgusted.

"Oh, right," Boscoe said while righting himself against the wall, "and you're a fucking beauty queen, you 'roid-rage monkey."

Dew shrugged. "That's what kind of shit you get when a demon fucks a wood nymph. A no-dick, water-brained fucktard that even Hell doesn't want."

"Yeah…well… Ow! Fuck!" Boscoe screamed, struggling to put his snapped leg back together. He stopped for a second and looked at Dew. "At least I can come and go as I please. I don't have to wait for some limp-dick jackhole like this to summon me," he said curtly, pointing at Travis.

Dew made a quick move at Boscoe, whose head shot back and slammed into the wall. Dew snickered at him. "You want to hit him again, T-man? I'll show you the sweet spot on him that'll make him wish he was a girl. Even though with what he's packing he might as well be one. Ain't that right, Boscoe, ya little *bitch*?" Dew walked up to Boscoe, his giant dick in hand and started whapping Boscoe on top of his head with it. "Betcha wish ya had one of these bad boys, huh, Bosc? Ya peanut-dicked mother fucker."

Boscoe's lips pursed tight while his slit-nostrils flared under from heavy breathing. Travis just knew Boscoe was blasting Dew the best fuck-you-and-die look a creature with no eyes could manage.

Travis contemplated Dew's offer, but shook his head. "No, maybe later."

Travis managed a controlled stumble to the bed and sat down hard on its edge. "How did he know? I mean she was in there with him..." Travis was shaking his head, so confused.

Dew looked at Boscoe and said, "You move and you know what'll happen, right?"

Boscoe grunted disgustedly, "Oh, I don't know... You'll stick me up your ass?"

"Bingo," Dew said happily and gave Boscoe another quick slap on the head with his dick. Then he let it go and the behemoth member retracted so far up into Dew's groin that he looked like a giant, evil-demon Ken doll, smooth as plastic. Travis stared in disbelief.

"I'm a grower not a show-er," Dew said casually. "Boscoe here is a show-er, only you don't know it." Then he let out a belly laugh and plopped himself down on the bed next to Travis. Travis popped into the air at least a foot.

When Travis righted himself, Dew explained.

"Everyone that comes to Painfreak has wants and needs and no matter how fucked up they are there is someone or something here to help them get what they want. Because ole Boscoe here hasn't got any useful tackle down there he has to get his kicks in other ways. Boscoe here feeds on misery and sorrow. He can get deep into your memories and manipulate what he finds in there to cause the kind of despair he needs to get off. It sucks, but there are people who get off on being miserable. And even though he is typically a worthless piece of shit, he serves a purpose to some, which is why he is allowed in here."

"Yeah, but I didn't ask for that," Travis said, still confused.

"Eh, things get fucked up sometimes. You order a hooker to your room and you think you're getting an Asian butterfly only to find your butterfly's packin' a springroll."

Boscoe huffed, "Nice."

Dew reached down and grabbed one of Travis' shoes and whipped it at Boscoe catching him square in the face. "Shut it!"

"Mother fucker! You are such a prick," Boscoe cried, rubbing his face. "And you owe me another soul mirror. That thing was expensive."

Dew let out an amused grunt. "Yeah, right. Why don't you learn how to use your fucking power properly and you wouldn't need one of those. You're such an impotent little shit."

## DADDY DEMON'S DAY OUT

Then Dew tossed a thumb in Boscoe's direction. "Most sorrow eaters worth a shit can just get into someone's mind and make people see them as whatever they want without the need for any supernaturally charged assistance. But not ole Boscoe here. He's got to rely on a soul mirror to channel the thoughts into something he can get off on. Pathetic."

"Yeah, well, at least my daddy still talks to me."

Travis didn't know what had happened but it got real hot in the room. *Really* hot. He could feel the bed start to shake. Travis found himself moving...*fast!*

"Watch the big guy," Boscoe said cheerily, "he's gonna blow."

And it did seem like he was indeed "gonna blow." The demon had gone a dark crimson and Travis could swear steam was coming out of various places on Dew's body.

"You ever want to piss-off an old school demon, just mention daddy," Boscoe laughed. Travis wondered if the little thing had a death wish. But he wondered from across the room.

Dew slowly stood and turned to Boscoe. But instead of showing fear, Boscoe just laughed louder at Dew. "Let me guess, you're gonna shove me up your ass?"

"Oh, you can bet on it," Dew said through gritted teeth. And he started toward Boscoe.

Boscoe didn't flinch. In fact, he seemed calmer than he had been since being pulled out of the mirror. "But I think *they* may have something to say about that."

Shadows filled the room in a wave of chilling wisps. They swirled around Travis' naked body, causing a massive attack of goosebumps. Then the shadows slipped further into the room, gathered and formed a solid wall of swirling grey smoke between Dew and Boscoe. And as Travis stared mesmerized at the churning mass it began to break apart. It split into four sections and each one spun itself into a miniature whirlwind, spinning, spinning, spinning. Travis grew dizzy and had to grab the wall behind him for support as the four twisters formed into four men—four very big and very mean looking men—all mirror images of one another.

The four men all brought up their right hands in unison. Dew stopped short, his anger visibly abating, but still clearly, totally pissed. "Is there a problem, Mr. Dewanal?" they all asked in a calm manor. The four voices echoed each other by just a split second, giving their already menacing presence an added creepiness.

Dew stood up straight, took a deep breath and let it out. "Just having a little disagreement with one of my distant cousins here."

"We have become aware of the situation here in regards to Mr. Boscoe. It would appear that he has overstepped his privileges and we will remove him, remind him of the rules and refuse his admittance for quite a while."

"Aw, shit, come on!" Boscoe yelled, not nearly as smug as he had been minutes ago. "It was a mis—"

But he stopped short when all four of the shadow men turned in unison and commanded him: "You *will* be silent."

Boscoe dropped his head and muttered to himself, "I'm just saying it was a mistake."

Dew's body color had changed back to its nondescript color and he laughed and clapped his hands together. "Boys, no trouble from me. I swear," he said holding his hands up in surrender. Then he turned to Travis, "T-man, get dressed." And Travis got dressed faster than he ever had in his life. Within seconds he had gathered his scattered clothing and even the shoe resting next to Boscoe and was fully clothed and standing next to Dew. The four shadow guards stood motionless.

"T-man and me are just gonna go ahead and blow out of here and let you tend to *Mr. Boscoe* here," Dew said, the sarcasm dripping. "Let me just make a door and we'll be on our way." Dew moved around the wall of shadow guards, about three feet from Boscoe, extended his claw up and placed one of his talons high up on the wall, poked his nail into the sheetrock and pulled it down. The wall responded like flesh, splitting apart, the edges of the incision puckering up and out. Behind the cut lay a void of deep crimson.

"There," Dew said proudly. "That'll do her." Then turning to Travis, "T-man, after you."

Travis didn't like this cordial Dew. This wasn't the demon he had come to know over the past couple of hours. It was kind of skeeving him out, but he moved forward anyway, stopped short of just walking right into the bloody hole, tossing it a skeptical look.

"Go for it, man. It's cool. I'll be right behind you," Dew assured.

So Travis placed a hand on the edge of the fleshy fissure. It felt like warm meat that seemed to suck his hand into it and made Travis shudder, but he closed his eyes and stepped through the gap.

Dew turned to the four shadow guards. "Sorry to have bothered you boys." And he began backing into the hole. "Wouldn't want to ruin any future fun I might have here by getting banned, so I'll just head on out."

The four guards all nodded at Dew as he entered the hole he had created. Dew continued backing into the red void and once he was all the way in it started to heal itself, the cut fusing back together at the top and bottom. The two ends grew closer and closer and were about to meet when Dew's upper body shot back out of the remaining gap. "Sorry, boys, I'm gonna be needing this." His arm lashed forward and his claw wrapped itself around Boscoe's head with a firm grip and yanked. With a horrified *squeal* Boscoe was being pulled through the air and into the closing hole in the wall.

"*Shiiiiiii…*" was all the shadow guards heard as Boscoe disappeared behind the now closed wall-wound. They all gave the wall an irritated squint, shrugged, then tilted their heads slightly as if hearing someone calling them. They all collapsed into swirling shadows once again and took off out of the room.

«« — »»

Travis found himself standing on a field of flesh. He turned in place, looking around him and knew instantly where he was. But it wasn't quite what he expected. When he finished his circle he found Dew standing there with a squirming Boscoe dangling from his claw.

"Let me go, you prick!" Boscoe squealed.

Travis ignored him and looked at Dew instead. "Guess this is Hell, huh?"

Dew looked around absently. "Sort of."

"Kind of stinks." Travis wrinkled his nose at the smell. It wasn't horrible, like a rotting carcass, but definitely had a meaty and earthy odor.

"Yeah, well, what did you expect, cinnamon and apples?"

Travis turned his back to Dew and stared out over the downward sloping flesh field, its raw, red hills extending far off into the distance until it met a mountain of tangled bone. Travis noticed something even more odd about the ground, as if being made of flesh wasn't strange enough. He stared with fascination as the ground seemed to rise and fall ever so slightly. Like it was breathing. "Okay, that's creepy."

Travis then shrugged and turned back to Dew. "Not as hot as I thought it would be," he said casually.

"Well, like I said, it's *sort of* Hell. More like Hell's Home Depot. Everyone has their own vision of Hell, their own preconceived ideas. This is where the building materials for each individual Hell comes from."

Travis raised his left eyebrow—he could never raise the right one for some reason. "Really? So everyone who goes to Hell has their own personal Hell then? No huge pit of bodies writhing in agony? No demons with pitchforks skewering the damned?"

"Sure… Well, used to be that way. There were a lot of pits, a lot of pain, anguish, torment, screaming, gnashing of teeth and all that shit, and it had all been customized." Dew grew animated, moving his hands about the air, Boscoe jerking around like a rag doll. "Everyone's Hell was like a little play with its own set and cast of characters. One guy's Hell may be spending eternity surrounded by screaming kids with snot covered noses. Another might go more old school with the demons and shit."

Travis nodded. "So that's when you get called in?"

Dew shook his head. "Not anymore. I mean, we did at first, when people started thinking about Hell as a real place and started coming down here, but thanks to Christianity, Hell started getting busy real quick. It was fun back in the old days, but man, the hours got worse and worse. So someone, don't remember who, came up with the idea for the personalized Hells." Dew motioned to the landscape. "Then they formed all this shit to help create them." Dew paused and seemed to be lost in thought. Then he quietly said, "But it's all different now. Hell has changed. The boss has bigger plans now."

Travis could tell there were some serious issues under the surface of what Dew was saying. But he figured it was best to let it go. It wasn't his business and if Dew wanted to tell him he would. "So you all kind of retired?" Travis asked trying to bring Dew back to the here and now.

Dew shook himself out of his thoughts. "Yeah, kind of had to. There aren't that many of us. I mean true demons are The Fallen and it's not like there were millions of us. Just too many people coming here for us to handle. We couldn't breed fast enough to keep up with demand. I mean, just think about it, if you believe in Hell and that any sin you do will make you end up there, then you're *going* to end up there."

Travis shook his head, trying to wrap his brain around what Dew was saying. "So all the people who believe in Hell end up here because of their guilt?"

"Not *all,* but most yeah. Most Christians end up down here. Almost no one goes to Heaven except for Jews."

"Ha, really?"

"Yeah, and fucking crazy bastards who think they are righteous. Cult leaders, mass murderers killing in the name of God who think they will go to Heaven because they are doing God's work. They believe it so it happens."

Travis stared wide-eyed at Dew. "Shit."

"Yep, it's a bitch. You should see the look on some priests' faces when they end up down here. Fucking priceless."

"I bet," Travis agreed. Then he thought some more and noticed Boscoe again. "What about things like him? Couldn't you just make a lot more demons to handle the work?"

Dew shook Boscoe some more bringing another squeal from him. "Tried at first. Couldn't breed enough to keep up with demand. So we went to the raw material idea. Plus, you ever see some of the female demons?" Dew shuddered. "I'd rather fuck Boscoe here."

"You wish," Boscoe said disgustedly.

Dew shook Boscoe a couple of times. "Shut up, buttplug." Then to Travis, "We have a lot of halfbreed children like dipshit here. Got to give his daddy credit, wood nymphs are fucking hot. Too bad you end up with fucktards like this." Dew held Boscoe up to his face. "Speaking of which…spelunking time."

Boscoe doubled his squirming effort. "No, Dew. Don't, please. We're family!"

"I know, I know. That's why you're going in the backdoor and not the long way."

"Oh, shit!"

"Exactly," Dew laughed. Then he proceeded to snap all of Boscoe's limbs, which left Boscoe a screaming mess. Dew flipped the half-breed upside down and held him by his broken legs. "Upsy daisy," Dew said and launched Boscoe high up in the air. He shot Travis a quick grin. "Watch this."

Dew jumped up did an impressive half flip, came down on his hands, arms spread wide, his legs leaning forward, but apart and opened his asshole…wide. Travis was stunned. Boscoe's scream of *Nooooooo,* snapped Travis from his asshole-gaze and looked up just in time to see the spindly demon-nymph descend rapidly into Dew's gaping butthole. As Boscoe disappeared, his scream grew distant as if he was falling into an endless pit. The sound was cut off when Dew slammed his hole closed, pushed off the ground, did a half-backflip and landed on his feet. He slapped his hands together and rubbed them. "That's that."

"Can't he just crawl out of there?" Travis asked somewhat confused, partially wanting to know the answer and partially *not*.

"Not anytime soon. It's like another fucking world in there. My ass is vast and far-reaching," Dew said proudly. "It knows no end."

"Awesome," was all that Travis could say.

"You fucking know it." Then Dew let out that big laugh Travis had grown used to, but now there was something missing from it. Dew seemed different since the scene at Painfreak. Something in his demeanor had changed. Travis could sense that Dew was trying to be the same, but it was an act. Travis just knew that what Boscoe said to Dew back in the room had struck a nerve and cut deep. But Travis decided not to pursue it. And before he could think anymore about it Dew said, "Okay, T-man, time to take care of your business. "

Travis shook himself out of his thought. "Uh, okay."

"So you want to find the guy who killed your wife and do something nasty to him?"

Travis was shocked and stood there jaw hanging. He stuttered a bit before saying, "How did you…"

Dew moved up next to Travis and placed his bigass arm around Travis' shoulders. "Give me a break, T-man. I know everything about you. When you summon a demon, you become an open book."

Travis flashed Dew an angry look. "Then why the hell did…"

"Relax, man. I wanted to have some fun. I don't get out of Hell all that often. Gotta take advantage when I can."

"Damnit!"

"Easy, boy. It's your time now. Hold on, we're going for another spin." And Dew pulled Travis in tight and they were gone in a flash.

«« — »»

## DADDY DEMON'S DAY OUT

Although this was the second time in hours Travis had traveled by Dew's black vortex express, it wasn't much better than the first time. At least Travis didn't pass out and go into another replay of the past. He couldn't really handle another episode reminding him of his wife and her terrible death at the hand of a madman…

…a madman he would soon confront and end his half-century long campaign for revenge. Soon he could put an end to his nightmares. Soon he could rest.

«« — »»

They emerged from the darkness into the entrance of an alley off a large but quiet street. Travis shook off the effects of the trip and followed Dew out onto the brightly lit curb. Buildings towered on all sides. Travis couldn't tell where exactly they were: New York, Chicago? Whatever. It didn't matter as long as the journey ended here, tonight.

There was electricity in the air. The hair all over his body stood at attention leaving Travis feeling like he was covered in ants. He looked around, wondering what the hell—

"FUCK! GET DOWN!" Dew screamed and shoved Travis hard, back into the dark alley. Dew watched Travis hit the ground and spun back toward the street and raised his head. It took Travis a second to rebound and roll onto his back, pushing himself up just in time to see Dew's body expand. His skin turned black, his muscles rippled as if preparing himself. The air changed and the ground began to vibrate beneath his ass. Travis' eyes opened wide in pure fear. *What the fuck is going on?* He looked past Dew's shoulder. Then…utter stillness for a split second…

…then…

Dew spread his arms wide, his muscles bulging to almost bursting his skin and he yelled, "*Aiiigghhh!!!*"

**FWOOOSH!! BOOOOM!!!**

A flash of light completely obliterated the top floor of the building across from Dew. Travis was blinded but somehow his survival instincts kicked in and he launched himself at Dew's feet, and into the shelter of the demon's rock-hard body.

Within seconds the first of the debris started landing around them. Large chunks of twisted metal and stone wrapped in flame descended upon them, Dew batting them away like he was swatting at flies. The barrage of burning bits of building was relentless and came at them for what seemed an eternity. Travis stayed huddled behind Dew, praying it would end soon. And *soon* it did. The downpour of destruction gave way to a cloud of dust and smoke that enveloped Travis and Dew in its choking embrace.

Travis began hacking.

"Hold on, man. I got it," Dew assured and then

# DADDY DEMON'S DAY OUT

Travis heard the demon inhale. It lasted for a minute and then the sound of a wind tunnel erupted from Dew as he let out a burst of air that cleared the debris cloud from around them. Travis's choking subsided a little and he managed to stand.

"What...what the...hell was that?" Travis shakily asked, still very afraid.

"Shhhhh!" Dew commanded. "Something is wrong. Very wrong." He stood taller and smelled the air. "Something is here. Something I haven't sensed in a very long time." Then his shoulders slumped a little. "Oh shit," he said softly.

Dew turned and looked straight at Travis, his eyes, both very visible through the lumpy mass of his face. And in those eyes Travis saw fear. Pure...fear.

Travis backed up a little, concern lining his face. "What?" Travis was on the verge of sheer panic. "What?"

"What the fuck have you done?" Dew said, menace in his voice.

Travis backed up more. "I-I-I don't... What are you talking..."

But before he could finish he saw Dew's claw flash forward to close over his face. Travis' words were muffled. Dew pushed Travis a little further into the shadows but still close enough to the street so they could see.

"Quiet," Dew hissed. Then he looked around cautiously, afraid. "I don't want it to see us."

They watched as the dust cloud settled to the ground. Burning paper fireflies danced through the air with falling black ash. They continued looking up, up and up until they found the smoking remains of the office building's top floor. Through the smoke and fire, twisted limbs of metal stabbed the night's sky. The building settled in a loud series of creaks and moans accented with the harsh crashing sound of falling glass.

"Don't move," Dew ordered.

Travis did as he was told. But Dew's massive claw tightened even more over the small man's face and Travis began slapping Dew's arm, mumbling in panic beneath the demon's grip. "Shhh. I don't want to be seen." But suddenly Dew let go, realizing it was already too late. They *had* been seen.

Travis remained silent, looking up, confused. Then he saw it—something plummeting through the night sky...

*down, down, down...*

...to the street—the street right in front of the alley where Travis and Dew now stood.

«« — »»

Travis didn't think Dew could get any more tense, but he did just that. Dew crouched down as if preparing for an attack.

It quickly became apparent that the falling figure

was that of a man. He seemed to fall for a long time. He remained upright, his feet approaching the ground rapidly. For an instant Travis thought that dropping off the side of the building had been a bad idea. This guy was gonna be splattered meat in a few seconds. But at the same time Travis just *knew* that wasn't going to happen. And he was right.

As the man reached and then fired past the 15th floor his back erupted. A soul-shattering cry filled the night sky and Travis heard Dew mutter, "Fuck me!" But Travis kept his eyes trained on the man. He continued to scream as a golden light encircled his body. And as he drew closer to the ground he seemed to grow larger. But Travis soon realized it wasn't the man himself getting bigger, but something behind him. *Are those…* Travis' thought got cut short as he realized that, yes, what he was seeing was real and that the man had sprouted a set of large, white wings.

The winged man's descent slowed, but it was obvious he didn't know how to use the wings on his back. He wobbled around in the air. His drop became more of an agitated jig as he jerked around, his wings seemingly *trying* to slow him down. The wings twisted and soon the man was leveling out about 50 feet above the ground. He zoomed to the left, heading down the street away from Dew and Travis. But Dew remained crouched and ready.

The wings twisted again and gave a big flap and the

man quickly changed direction and headed straight toward them. The wings continued to flap and the man flew down toward the street. His angle of descent was a sharp one and he hit the ground hard, tucking himself into a tight ball and rolling once he landed.

Travis winced as he saw the man hit the street. *Oh, shit!* he thought. He half expected Dew to say something smartass, but the demon remained still, his eyes following the rolling, winged man as he tumbled past them.

The man came to rest on his stomach about 30 feet from the alley. He lay there motionless for a few moments. Then he showed some signs of life as his wings twitched. Some soft moans emanated from the feathery mess. And very slowly the man pushed himself up and leaned back until he was kneeling, his upper body slumping to the right. His body shook in sharp spasms as he tried to gather enough air. The spasms subsided as he took a deep breath and exhaled, gaining control over his breathing once again. The man then sighed and stood. He was a little wobbly at first and stumbled over to the side of the street and grabbed hold of a lamppost for support. He hung his head, shaking it from side to side.

Travis wanted Dew to do something. Wanted the man to do something. Wanted *someone* to do *something*. So he did. Travis took a hesitant step toward the man. "Jesus, man. Are you alright?" he asked meekly.

Dew put his hand on Travis' chest, shaking his head.

# DADDY DEMON'S DAY OUT

The stranger straightened up and twisted his neck to look at his newfound appendages. He reached up with his right hand and pensively touched the left wing as if it were a strange dog that would bite him at any second. After a few soft strokes of the wing he relaxed some. He dropped his hand and flapped each wing separately; then both at the same time. Slowly at first, but he grew more confident in his control over them and began to flap them faster.

Travis was sure he realized the guy's feet had left the ground before the guy did. But it only took a few seconds before he looked down and noticed he was hovering about a foot above the street.

"Would you look at this shit," he said in awe of this new development. He flapped a little more and rose a couple of more feet into the air. Then he slowed his wings and settled to the ground again.

The guy looked at Dew and Travis. "That's new," he said. Then excitedly, "Fucking *sweeeeeet!*" He hunched his shoulders and rolled them a bit and then like *that*, the wings were gone. "Those should come in handy."

He tried to smooth himself out and brush himself off, but the crash landing had done some serious damage to his clothes. Or maybe it was the explosion. Either way, the guy was a mess. But he finished fussing with himself then took a couple of steps toward Dew and Travis.

Dew let a low growl rumble out. The man stopped. His eyes narrowed as he took in Dew. "Better leash your mutt here, boy," he said to Travis while keeping his eyes trained on the demon.

"He's not my master," Dew said, menace tainting his words.

The man's eyes went wide as he grinned. "It speaks. Neat." Then he adopted a more relaxed stance. "What the hell are you, ugly?"

Dew's growl intensified. Travis decided to intervene.

"Alright, guys, easy." He moved between the two, putting his arms up. "Let's go easy here. No need for chest thumping."

Travis turned his back to Dew and faced the man. "Look, we're here for something and I'd really like to get on with it. So what say we just put our dicks away and go about our separate business."

The man shrugged. "Fine with me. I got some serious shit to get started on anyway." But he paused, suddenly curious. "What are you looking for?" he asked.

Travis started to explain, but hesitated and simply stated, "Revenge."

The guy's eyes lit up. "Ain't that a co-inky-dink… Me too. Who pissed you off?"

Travis paused again, but for a reason he didn't understand, went ahead and told the guy. "We're looking for someone…"

He could feel Dew's hot breath on his back as the demon inhaled and exhaled heavily. "Travis… Don't."

But Travis went on. "A guy."

"Oh yeah? What'd this guy do?" asked the guy.

"He killed my wife."

The guy nodded as if he understood it all. "That's a bitch." Then tossing a thumb in Dew's direction. "And what is that?"

Travis turned sideways so he could see the guy and Dew. "This's Dew. He's helping me."

"That's one butt-ugly tracking hound."

"Fuck you," Dew spat.

The guy laughed.

"You don't seem too concerned," wondered Travis aloud. "I mean if there were a demon standing there growling at me I'd be a little concerned."

The guy seemed to mull this over a bit. Then he nodded. "Yeah, you'd think, right? But it's been one of those nights. Not much is surprising me anymore. Besides—"

"I smell the Divine on you," Dew interrupted.

The guy smiled. "Oh yeah?"

"Not pure. Tainted."

"Buddy, you can say that again," the guy said and started laughing again.

"Infected with humanity." Disgust riddled Dew's words.

"Uh, yeah...*no*. I wouldn't say that." The guy seemed offended. "Whatever humanity I had has been fucked out of me with a giant *heavenly* dildo." The man gave Dew a wink. "But I guess you'd know about that, right?"

"Don't assume you know me." Dew shook his head slightly. "I was tricked by a liar full of hollow promises. But the decisions were mine to make and I hold *myself* responsible for what I am."

This time the man's words held disgust, "How fucking noble. So what? No revenge for you tonight, Dew?" The guy grew animated and began pacing, arms flailing about. "I mean, come on, man. Look around you. Can't you feel it? Revenge is in the air." Then he turned to Travis. "You...what's your name?"

"Travis."

"Look at Travis here. He's all ready for revenge. Some eye for an eye. Tit for tat, and *all* that." He turned to face Dew. "Aren't you pissed? Don't you want some*one*, some*thing*, to pay for what you've become."

Dew didn't answer right away as he thought about what the man was saying. "What I am is of no concern to you," Dew said softly.

The guy shook his head. "I didn't think a demon would be such a pussy."

Dew jumped forward, coming within reaching distance. Travis just barely got out of the way in time. "Check your tone with me half-breed."

Travis watched the guy expecting him to fall back. But he held his ground and just smiled at Dew. Travis moved forward, but not enough to get in between the two. "Okay, easy guys. Come on, calm down. We all have our reasons for what we're doing. Knock off the name calling."

Travis looked at the guy. "Look… What's your name?"

"Well, there's a good question. It was Mal for a long time, but recent events have me wondering just who and what I am."

"Okay, okay. Mal then. I don't want anyone to get hurt here…"

The guy's hand moved quickly to his pocket, disappearing for a second before reemerging with a knife. "I bet mister demon there won't be trying anything on me too soon."

Travis saw Dew back up two paces when the knife was pulled. "How did you—?" Dew hissed.

"This?" The guy moved the blade through the air. "Little gift from my mentor. Learned some interesting things about it just a little while ago. You may have seen our work." The man flicked his head at the building behind him…the one missing the top floor.

"That isn't meant for you," Dew stated flatly. "That shouldn't exist."

"Yeah, well, take a good look. It *does*."

Travis stared at the knife cutting through the air, streetlight reflecting off its brilliant surface. There was no doubt there was power there—a *lot* of power. The air became electrified. Travis felt a prickling sensation cover his body.

Mal stopped waving the knife. "And let me tell you something, my demon friend, it fucking works too."

"Who?" Dew asked.

"Back there? Oh, maybe an old friend of yours." Mal rolled his shoulders casually. "Guy named Jericho. You know him?'

Dew nodded, "Once."

Mal laughed. "Well, best pay some respects now. Because he got a little prick from my friend here." And Mal poked the knife out toward Dew. Dew backed away another few feet.

Travis never took his eyes off the knife. "What is that?"

"Tell him, Dew. You seem to recognize it."

Dew kept his eyes trained on the tip of the blade as if waiting for it to start talking. "The Blade of Undoing. Something that shouldn't be... Not anymore."

"As you can see, it does. And my guess is that it will do to you what it just did to our angel friend back there. So my advice, Dew... Stay the fuck away from me."

Travis forced himself to look away from the gleaming blade. "Uh, y-y-yeah. We should go. We still have business." Then he looked at Dew. "What say we go and look for our guy and let Mal get on with his...whatever."

"No," said Dew coldly.

Mal arched an eyebrow at the demon and braced himself, holding the knife steady in front of him.

## DADDY DEMON'S DAY OUT

Travis could feel massive tension flood over the scene. He needed to end this and get Dew away from Mal. The guy was obviously dangerous and there was a hell of a lot more going on here than Travis could fathom or wanted to for that matter. Mal's problems were his and didn't involve them. So... "Dew, let's go."

"No," the demon said again.

Travis was growing more nervous. "Look... You said you'd help me. You promised. You said we'd find the guy who killed Sally. Now, let's go find him."

Dew looked at Travis and very quietly said, "We already have."

«« — »»

Stunned silence blanketed the street and the three figures standing atop it. The already tense situation was perilously close to its snapping point as breaths found themselves trapped within heaving chests. Time stood still as Mal and Travis tried to grasp the gravity of Dew's words.

"Shit," was all Mal could say as realization set in. He took a step back, shaking his head as he moved.

Travis stood stone-still as he tried to wrap his head around Dew's words. He looked to the demon for any signs that what he had just said was just a joke—a sick fucking joke. But Travis' hopes were crushed with one short, quick nod from Dew, whose eyes held a mixture of sympathy and concern. But was it concern for Travis or for the demon himself? Travis' face went slack as the reality of the situation sank in. He had come to the end of his long, long journey. He had committed countless atrocities, all in his quest for vengeance. He had literally gone to *Hell* and back to get to this point—to find the *man* responsible for the death of his one and only true love. Only this *man* wasn't a *man* at all. Travis wasn't sure what Mal was, but what he did know was that the demon he had summoned from the depths of Hell itself, this huge, full-blooded, scary as hell monster, was afraid of Mal. Or at least afraid of the power that Mal wielded in his hand.

*No, no, no,* Travis said to himself over and over. He turned slowly in place until he was facing Mal, whose face held a wary look of shock and surprise.

Mal held his hands up. "Look, man, I don't…"

Travis narrowed his eyes at Mal. "Shut up," he ordered in a low, rough voice.

"Seriously, I have no idea…"

Travis' arm shot forward, his index finger pointing accusingly at Mal. "I SAID, SHUT THE FUCK UP!"

Mal did.

Travis was trembling, his confusion giving way to sheer anger. "Did you kill my wife?"

Mal looked genuinely lost. "I don't know, man. I've killed a lot of people."

"I don't care about 'a lot of people.' I only care about one," Travis stated.

Mal shrugged his shoulders. "How am I supposed to know? I mean, it's possible. Shit…"

Travis dropped his arm and reached inside his jacket. Mal stiffened, preparing for an attack. Dew did the same. But when Travis' hand reemerged it held a photo. A very old, faded, worn, black and white photo of a woman. He held it out to Mal. "Look at it. LOOK…AT…IT! Do you recognize her?"

Mal's eyes went wide at the realization that, yes, yes he did recognize her. He could never forget her.

He had been given his first order: *"You are to go into the school. Find room 315. Enter. Then dispense with the teacher. A Mrs. Sally Burnsfield."* And that's exactly what Mal had done. She was his first kill, his first taste of the salvation promised him. A promise that turned out to be a lie and now that taste had become very bitter indeed.

Travis saw the look on Mal's face and knew instantly that Dew had not lied. This was indeed the man who had killed Sally. "You fucking bastard. You killed the only person I ever loved."

For the first time in a long while Mal actually felt bad about something he had done. He didn't know this guy trembling in front of him. But he knew he had done the man wrong. But it had been so long ago—decades. Mal hadn't thought about it in years. Hadn't thought about his first kill, and the teacher's hot blood running from her slit neck over his hand and down his arm. And he really didn't want to think about it. He brought his head up and looked Travis right in the eyes. "I'm sorry," was all he could say.

Travis was shaking, barely able to contain his rage. "Sorry? You're fucking sorry?" he spat. "That's fucking great." Then he threw his arms up in mock surrender. "Okay, all better then. Guess I'll just go home now."

Mal watched Travis as he ranted and wondered how this guy could even be standing here right now. He had to be at *least* eighty years old.

"Do you know how long I've been looking for you?"

Mal honestly didn't know for sure. So he just said, "A long time."

Travis let out a slightly maniacal laugh. "A long time? Try forty fucking years."

That's some dedication Mal thought. "How did you even know I'd still be alive?"

"I didn't care. I just wanted to know your name. If I couldn't get you, I'd get your family, friends, anything you cared about. But no one could help me. NO ONE! No trace of you. Nothing. You just fucking disappeared."

*Gregory*, Mal thought. He had made it so easy for Mal to do what he did. Cleaned up every trail. Made him invisible. And while Mal was briefly lost in thought Travis had moved to within inches of Mal's face.

"I had to find other ways. I had to do shit no one should just to get to this day and all you can say is 'I'm sorry'?"

## DADDY DEMON'S DAY OUT

Even though Mal could understand Travis' anger, he didn't like this man up in his face like this. So he shoved his face to where he was almost touching noses with Travis. "Yeah! That's all I can fucking say! I...am...sorry! What the fuck do you want from me?"

Travis stopped shaking, leveled his eyes at Mal and quietly said, "I want you dead."

Mal laughed to himself. *I bet*, he thought. "Oh yeah."

"And now that Dew here knows who you are, once we get finished with you we're going to track down your family—everyone you love—and destroy them too."

That made Mal laugh out loud right in Travis' face. "My family? Ha! Not if I get to them first. And I don't think your guard dog or especially..." Mal poked Travis in the chest, "...*you* are going to stop me—" And Mal ended his declaration with a solid headbutt to Travis' nose.

Travis dropped to his knees in an instant, blood exploding from his nose. Dew moved forward a couple of paces. Mal brought the knife up to remind Dew why he had been keeping his distance to begin with.

"Back off, my man. You sure you want to tangle with..."

*ooof!*

Mal felt the pain no man ever wants to feel shoot up through his body as Travis' uppercut to Mal's balls brought tears to the assassin's eyes. "Aw...you...fuck...,"

Mal wheezed between gasps for air as he doubled over, one hand covering his now throbbing sack.

Travis looked up defiantly and started to rise, cupping his mashed face. "STHFFIT! You bwoke my fwoonckin'—"

The knife cut off Travis in more ways than one. Before he could even get up, Mal's knife hand came up and slashed through the air leaving a thin crimson line across Travis' neck. Everything stopped. No motion, no sound, just the utter stillness of an endless instant. Then…a curtain of blood dropped from the widening wound.

Travis fell back on his haunches, his face a mask of disbelief. He choked and struggled to speak, his words a rough, gurgling mess. "No—no—no." Tears exploded from his eyes and ran down his cheeks.

Dew came up behind Travis and crouched down letting the little man lean back into one of his massive arms. He brought his face down next to Travis' head. "I'm sorry, T-man."

Travis looked up at Dew, his eyes wide with a mixture of confusion, shock and horror. He had made it this far. Why wasn't Dew helping? Why did he just let this happen? "Why?" he croaked.

Dew hung his head, shaking it. "There is something bigger going on here, man. Something bigger than you or I. Something more than just your revenge." Dew looked at Mal who was on one knee, still cradling his groin, moaning. Then he turned back to Travis. "But I will find out, I promise you that."

Travis could feel his blood soaking through his shirt and coating his chest. His vision grew blurry. "He killed Sally. Please…," he begged.

"No," Dew said softly. "He was just the weapon."

Travis struggled to get up, to kill his wife's murderer, to finish what he started. But his body wouldn't cooperate. His struggles amounted to no more than some pathetic spasms. Eventually he stopped trying but his body continued to convulse in a fit of sobs.

Travis closed his eyes and fell back into Dew once again. Dew leaned down and whispered something to the dying man and then waited. After a few seconds Dew asked, "Do you see it?"

Travis gave a weak nod and in a choked whisper said, "Yeah."

"Good," Dew replied and quickly snapped Travis' neck.

Dew stayed there with Travis nestled into the crook of his arm for a minute. The demon was lost in thought. Too much was happening and Dew was losing himself amid the chaos. This was supposed to have been a night of fun. But ever since he'd heard Travis screaming from inside that room in Painfreak he had this gnawing feeling the night had turned to shit and wasn't going to get any better.

This should have been simple. Some fun, then give the guy what he wanted, then return to The Pit and wait for some other revenge-crazed tool to summon him. After all, he was the demon of revenge, and so many have been hurt and want payback. Dew was the last hope for many of them. So many people have tried to summon him: hurt husbands, betrayed wives, bruised egos, etc. But so few actually called forth Dew. Most of them were jackasses, but Dew always gave them what they wanted in the end. No tricks, no false promises, not like the bastard who fooled him so long ago and led him down a path of lies—a path leading so far from the one place Dew wanted to be but would never see again. He wished he could make Lucifer pay for what he had done. But the sad thing was, even the demon of *revenge* couldn't make the devil pay for his lies and betrayals. *What a fucking bitch,* Dew thought. He sighed openly still lost in his thoughts until he felt a firm tap on his shoulder.

Dew snapped back into reality and found himself looking at Mal who appeared to have recovered from Travis' ball attack, although his face was glowing red and covered in sweat.

"So, big boy," Mal said, "we gonna get rough and tumble or is this over?"

"Back off," Dew stated coolly. And Mal did.

Dew stood up bringing Travis' limp body with him. He cradled the dead man in his arms and carried it over closer to the building Mal had dropped from. He laid

Travis down gently next to a large piece of rubble from the explosion. Then he turned around and headed back toward Mal.

Mal waited patiently, but was obviously on alert. Dew stopped a few feet from Mal. Mal gave a *what's up* motion toward Travis' body.

"It'll look like he got hit by a piece of building and that's what snapped his neck," Dew answered.

Mal nodded knowingly. "Gotcha. So back to my previous question…"

"Neither."

"How so?" Mal asked.

"We aren't going to fight and this is *far* from over. You have something you shouldn't and I wanna find out why."

"So what, you think we're partners now or something?"

Dew shrugged. "Or something."

Mal shook his head. "Look, man, you're all big and scary and shit and could probably come in handy bigtime, but I work alone."

Dew stood to his full height—a menacing sight indeed—and crossed his arms defiantly. "Not anymore you don't. I have a lot of questions I'd like answers to and I have a feeling those answers lie along your path, so I'm walking it with you. Besides, you want revenge. I am the demon of revenge. Seems like a perfect match."

Mal thought for a second then nodded. "Okay." Then

he looked around. "Seem odd to you that a building just blew up and there's no one around?"

"That's one of my questions. It would seem someone of power is working behind the scenes here, giving you enough time to get away."

"Gregory," Mal whispered.

"I don't know who that is exactly, but I'm sure I'll recognize him when I see him." Then Dew began to walk away from the building. "But I think we need to go."

Just then Mal heard the faint peal of sirens in the distance. "Shit."

Dew kept walking and Mal ran to catch up.

"What did you say to Travis back there before you…you know?" Mal asked.

Dew did not look back, but instead stayed focused on getting away from the scene behind them. "I told him to picture his wife and to make his own heaven. And when he did, I ended his life. Now he will be with her for eternity locked into a happy place where she was never murdered."

Mal found himself looking down at the ground as they walked. "You know… I… I really am sorry about that. It's the only thing I feel bad about. It was my first…"

"I don't want to know," Dew interrupted. "Doesn't matter. You were a weapon, manipulated. And I promised Travis I would find out who's pulling your strings."

"Pulled," Mal corrected.

"Pulled." Dew understood. "So, now we go find your *ex*-puppetmaster and get some answers."

"Just as long as I get to kill him," Mal stated seriously.

Dew gave an amused snort. "You're a cocky little fuck, ain't you?"

"Yeah, and I'll be even more so when I enter the gates of Heaven and start kicking everyone's angelic asses."

Dew found his breath stuck in his chest for an instance. He had planned on killing this fucker once he got some answers to his questions. But something told him that there was truth in the little killer's words. And if so, then maybe there was a chance that Dew would see his home once again. He calmed himself down without letting Mal see any change in him.

"So that's your plan?" Dew asked nonchalantly.

"Yep," Mal replied confidently.

"Guess I'll have to wait to kill you then."

"Fuckin' A!" Mal said without missing a beat.

The two walked into the night, the sound of sirens behind them and the promise of sweet revenge hanging heavy over the road before them.

The old man emerged from the shadows of the alley and took in the destruction. He had sensed the power and was drawn to it. He looked up, up and up at the decapitated building and felt sorrow for the loss of an old friend.

Something caught his eye and he watched as it descended from the sky slowly floating down, dancing on air currents.

The old man heard the sirens blaring long before the police car came speeding around the corner followed closely by a monstrous fire truck and even more emergency vehicles. But he didn't take his eyes from the sky. Instead, he remained stone still in the middle of the street even as the police car barreled toward him.

Shock crossed the face of the police officer as he realized someone was standing in the street amid the smoky debris. He only had a split second to act. He jerked the wheel hard and went into a sideways skid and out of the

## THE SLEEPERS AWAKEN

driver's side window he saw the fire truck hurtling toward him. The officer's eyes went wide with panic as he heard the red behemoth's tires squeal atop the pavement and saw smoke rise from the melting tires. All the officer could do was close his eyes and wait for the...

With a slight wave of his hand, the old man brought the potential disaster to a grinding halt. Everything around him went motionless and the harsh sounds of emergency vehicles were abruptly extinguished. Now it was just the old man and what he was watching drop out of the sky. He waited patiently and after a minute more he held out a hand and let the glowing white feather land oh so softly into it. He held it out before his face for some time, taking it in and a small tear ran down his wrinkled cheek. "I am sorry, Jericho. You deserved better than this. I had hoped for your assistance in the task before me. But I waited too long. I will make amends to you, old friend. This I promise." And with that the old man wiped the tear from his face with his coat sleeve then slowly opened his jacket and gently placed the feather inside a hidden pocket.

He closed his jacket, turned to the men and their vehicles frozen in time, all with expressions of panicked horror lining their faces. He sighed deeply and then was gone.

Neither the police officer nor the fire fighters in the cab of the fire truck knew what had happened. All they knew was that they had been a split second away from

catastrophe, but now they sat safely in their respective vehicles breathing heavy and letting nervous laughter drift out their windows.

The police officer, still shaking, was the first out of his car. The fire truck driver followed suit. They met in the middle of the street and exchanged anxious looks while shaking their heads. Neither knew what had happened. After a few more seconds of uncertainty, both men shook off the images of their deaths and went into action that years of training had worked into their DNA. They had a job to do.

Neither would ever mention what had just happened again. It was just too damn weird.

«« — »»

Harv's 24 Hour Diner — BEST EATS ON HIGHWAY 57. Of course Highway 57 was what the Johnsonians called it. It was actually 57th Street. Ran North to South between Johnson Rd. and Johnson Ave. Exactly three-tenths of a mile long or short, what have you.

Back in 1957, the Johnsonians, well 35 of the 127 of them, all God-fearing citizens, met to decide the name of the new street that would connect Johnson Rd. to Johnson Ave.

The meeting lasted exactly two hours, thirty-four minutes and twenty seconds. The minutes of the meeting will verify this, and they are exact. Jonnie Mae Willims

# THE SLEEPERS AWAKEN

kept the time as she was the only person in Johnson to have a stopwatch. This is the primary reason she was assigned the task as secretary of the meeting.

See, Jonnie Mae, whom everyone called Jamie, had recently received this watch from her uncle, Thomas Jay Willims. Thomas Jay, who everyone called Toe Jam, was in Switzerland "broadening his horizons."

So, now Thomas James Willims was exploring the world, and getting the hell away from Johnson, GA where everyone called him Toe Jam all because of Suzy Simmons who spoke with a lisp. Everyone in fourth grade had made fun of her lisp. One morning, Thomas had decided he would win points with the guys by ridiculing Suzy during roll call. When Miss Hanson, with the legs of a goddess and the face of a mule, called Suzy Simmons' name, Thomas quietly repeated her name as Suzy would say it. The name came out wet and silly, and Suzy retaliated quickly with a loud, "Shut the hell up, Toe Jam." No lisp, very clearly. Suzy would be sent to the principal's office, very proud. Thomas "Toe Jam" Willims would be scarred for life. Now he was in Switzerland where no one would call him Toe Jam, ever. And as far as anyone knew, he was the only Johnsonian to ever go to Europe just for the Hell of it.

Of course there was the Cratch boy back in '42, but he went with the Marines and never came back. And it was this reason that Mrs. Cratch, had offered up her opinion as to what the new road should be called.

Everyone at the meeting knew what she would say. "The Samuel Cratch Memorial Lane," she said with the dignity of a queen.

"We'll add that to the list, Mrs. Cratch," Mayor Trumble said with a patient smile.

And so it was added to the list just as The Samuel Cratch Community Center, The Samuel Cratch Park, The Samuel Cratch Public Library and countless other buildings, streets, etc. had been over the years. All submitted by Mrs. Cratch in the hopes of honoring her son who died saving a fellow soldiers in the time of war:

> Dear Mrs. Cratch,
>
> It is with much regret that I must inform you of the untimely passing of your son Samuel. We here in the 103 had come to know Samuel, who we called Scratch, as an excellent soldier and close friend. You will be proud to know that Samuel died while attempting to save a fellow Marine. It was this selfless act that proved your son a true Marine and American. We will miss Scratch, and share in your sorrow at this most unfortunate time.
>
> May God be with you.
>
> Sincerely yours,
> Major Timothy Hawkins
> United States Marine Corps
> Semper Fi

# THE SLEEPERS AWAKEN

The entire population of Johnson, at that time being 73, came out to Momma Cratch's house and joined her in mourning her brave son who died dutifully in battle.

Of course there was no battle. Or so the people of Johnson discovered when a fellow 103rd came to town to see where his buddy Scratch hailed from. Tommy Shimble had found himself at Sloppy Mike's Tavern on the west side of Johnson Avenue. Tommy had been there the night of Samuel Cratch's undignified demise. And after a few hours, a few beers, and a few shots of Jack, Tommy let everyone in the bar in on the story of Scratch's death.

Apparently, Corporal S. Cratch, better known as Scratch to his buddies, had been playing a rousing game of leap-frog with Gretchen, a two-hundred-thirty-pound Germanic blossom of a woman. And a prostitute. They, Scratch and three other soldiers of the mighty 103, had rented a room in a small inn, whose name was loosely translated by one of the mighty 103rd as The Bloated Pigmy. In this room, they had also rented the company of a few of Berlin's finest ladies of the evening. Four of them, with a combined weight pushing close to a half a ton. The boys were in for some fun.

Someone, after too many strong German beers, had the idea of playing leap-frog—naked. No one objected. The game lasted only five minutes, but to the Swedish husband and wife in the room below…well, you can imagine.

Anyway, Scratch's three buddies each had fallen into romantic entanglements with the large love of their choice. They rolled and writhed and oozed on the floor while Scratch was content with the oddity of being so far from Johnson, GA, in the middle of a quaint inn in Germany, playing leap-frog with an overly plump German prostitute. He continued to be content in his contentment.

Eventually, Scratch stood with a grunt and proceeded to mount Gretchen's wide backside, amazed at the dark hairy chasm of her ass, and propelled himself up and over. He landed hard, and felt the room spin around him, the beer in his stomach threatening to coat Gretchen's landing area. He steadied himself and prepared for Gretchen's bulk to press upon his young Georgian back.

Gretchen giggled as she squatted, placed her hands heavily upon the cute American GI's skinny ass and jumped.

The room spun again for Scratch, his right knee, which he hurt falling off a tractor when he was twelve, but lied about to the Marines because he thought it would never bother him, buckled, then snapped. He went down hard. Gretchen went down hard. There was another snap. The mighty soldiers of the 103 laughed, and Corporal Samuel Cratch, better know as Scratch to his buddies, collapsed with a broken spine under a mass of German flesh better known as Gretchen, passed out

## THE SLEEPERS AWAKEN

on top of Scratch. Everyone went back to sins of the flesh, and come the next morning, three of the mighty soldiers of the 103rd had a lot of explaining to do to Major Timothy Hawkins, United States Marine Corps—*Semper Fi*.

Everyone sat open-mouthed as they listened to Tommy. He had managed to down a few more shots of Jack and was feeling pretty good as he finished his story with a loud, "I swear to God, that is the whole truth and nothing but the truth." And just as he was about to finish with a resounding Stan Laurel nod, Joseph Hayes Josephs came up behind Tommy and cracked him in the skull with a pool cue. Tommy fell hard.

The people from Sloppy Mike's Tavern left Tommy Shimble alone and naked out on Highway 15 (it's a real highway, they didn't just call it that) with his wallet taped to his ass with duct tape and a note taped to his hairy chest that said, "Never come back!"

He never did.

The people in the bar that night knew Mrs. Cratch. Hell, everyone did. And they all loved her dearly. Every year in honor of her boy, Mrs. Cratch would throw a huge picnic. She was so proud of her son. And no one wanted to hurt her. So that's why Tommy Shimble was quietly escorted out of Johnson, GA.

But, as it is in small towns, everyone eventually found out about Samuel. But to their credit, they kept the truth from his mother. And she in turn kept throwing her picnics. And the townspeople all loved her, but for some reason couldn't bring themselves to honor her son, even to make an old woman happy. So it was when she proposed that the new road in Johnson be named for her son, it was voted down. And Mrs. Cratch, still with the dignity of a queen, smiled slightly and said, "Well, maybe next time." And those around her would nod and agree, that yes, maybe "next time" would get it.

And finally that "next time" came and this time it wasn't up for a vote. No, see Momma Cratch owned a lot of land. When she got too old to tend to the fields, she decided to sell off little parts of her land. With the money she received, Mrs. Cratch started a home for wayward girls—a place for runaways, homeless, pregnant women and prostitutes. She called it The Samuel Cratch Hospice.

After the dedication, Momma Cratch quietly snuck out the back, got in her car and drove to Atlanta where she got on a plane to Key West and never came back to Johnson, GA again.

*Johnson Bugle*, July 8th 1977

When asked where Mrs. Cratch had gone, Gretchen Krause, coordinating supervisor for the new Samuel Cratch Hospice, replied simply, "I don't know."

# THE SLEEPERS AWAKEN

«« — »»

So Momma Cratch finally got what she had wanted for so long. Not the library, nor the park, not even what was now Highway 127. None of those bore the name of Samuel Cratch.

But you see, none of that mattered to the old man, who was now sitting quietly in the far southern booth of Harv's 24-Hour Diner, Best Eats on Highway 127.

He was alternating from staring out the window at the dry and cracked red Georgia clay that made up Harv's parking lot, and a dry splotch of brownish goo on the sun-bleached Formica tabletop before him.

He was still reeling from his eye-opening, albeit brief, visit to New York City. He pulled the feather from his jacket and took in its beauty. He held it gently by the tip and with his other hand, ran the back of his fingers along the feather's silky smooth surface. He continued caressing the feather even as his gaze moved back to the window next to him. The old man just stared, lost in thought until he was shaken back to reality by the reflection of the waitress as she approached his table.

"You ready to order, hon?" she asked with a slight southern drawl. It was a low, sexy voice. Almost like a loud whisper. The old man stared at her reflection in the grimy window for a moment, then turned to her. Her short fire-red bob hair bounced once then settled as she came to a stop. He marveled at her beauty and thought to himself, *So lovely, even after all this time.*

He slowly turned toward her—read her nametag, Rose. He smiled at the name, knowing what her real name was and how it had only changed a little.

Rose was about to speak when she noticed the feather in the old man's hand. She was struck by its beauty. "That's beautiful," she whispered.

The old man nodded, "It is, isn't it?" Then he held it out toward her. "Would you like to hold it?"

Rose held her sight on the feather, but slowly shook her head, "No, I couldn't…"

"I insist," the old man said and held the feather out for Rose to take.

She reached out hesitantly, she didn't feel like she should touch it but her hand seemed drawn to the feather and she couldn't keep herself from taking it. As she delicately wrapped her fingers around the offered end of the feather, Rose's breath caught for a second. She looked into the eyes of the old man. Something touched her deep inside and she felt flushed with confusion. She tried to shake it off. She started to speak and stammered a bit, clearing her throat and continuing.

"What is… I…" she struggled for words, fear beginning to blend with the confusion.

The old man smiled and reached up and wrapped his hand around Rose's and pressed the feather deep into her grasp. Rose dropped her order pad. Tony, the cook, saw

# THE SLEEPERS AWAKEN

what was happening and warily moved to her rescue as he had done in the past, only this time he made it two steps before he froze, as did everything in the diner—everything except for Rose and the old man in the far southern corner booth.

Rose stood stone still, fear running through her blood. But only for a second, because the fear was soon flushed away with a feeling of euphoria. Something buried deep, deep inside her had been uncovered, rediscovered and was resurfacing.

"It's time…Rose…" the old man said soothingly, a very slight but patient smile on his face, "…time for you to awaken." And with that, the old man filled Rose with the images of eons past. He showed her all that was beauty and all that was pain—he showed her the war between Heaven and Hell. The memories flooded into Rose and she shed a tear for each of her brothers and sisters fallen in battle for…what? Nothing really. And she cried for each millennia of missed memories stolen from her by this man sitting before her now. And suddenly her anger for this man grew. She tried to shake his grip, but he held fast. And continued to fill her mind. This time it was a recent battle—one that involved God directly, one which didn't go His way. And she watched as God, lazy and weak, had been cast out of Heaven. She felt as though she should feel sorry for this old man, but couldn't. She finally shook his hold, or he let go, she wasn't sure. She stepped back, breathing heavily. Her face a mask of pain and sorrow painted with cheap running make-up. Rose took a couple of deep breaths, paused, eyes wide, and hauled off and punched God right in the side of the head.

«« — »»

It's not all despair and pain. In fact there isn't a lot of pain. Not anymore. Hell is no longer for suffering, it's for building. Hell is a city—a city that runs like any other city. It requires workers—souls—souls that would work for eternity to help build the biggest, grandest city in all creation. All in tribute to a vision and the one who came up with the vision...

Lord Lucifer was looking over the plans for a new section of Hell. It would be mostly housing. The workers' numbers were increasing. Souls were being had easily. Lucifer knew why, and could care less. He had heard the reports of the ousting of God from Heaven and he shrugged. He knew the battle for souls with the angels had subsided. Gabriel hated humans and wanted nothing to do with them and therefore there would be no more fighting for their souls. Of course there were some holdouts—some who were out on the lines still fighting the good cause, oblivious to the change of power, the change of plans. And this is why Lucifer kept troops out on the front lines, not so much to fight for souls, they were pretty much ending up here anyway. No, he kept

# THE SLEEPERS AWAKEN

troops out there to keep an eye on Heaven's soldiers who didn't give up. Lucifer needed to keep an eye on them. Let them keep fighting. It was a pointless task on the angels' part. So when the time comes that all the angels are called home, Lucifer would then bring his troops back and train for a different task. But he also knew he could never let his guard down. His brothers and sisters above were treacherous beings—as evident by the ousting of their own maker.

For now, things must go on. He had a city to run, to build. His city, his vision, his world. Not God's, not the human's, not the angel's…his. *This* is what concerned him most.

«« — »»

Gabriel sat quietly upon the throne of Creation. He rubbed his eyes and sighed. He had done it. He had achieved what he had wanted to for so long. So much planning and time and effort. And for nothing. It wasn't hard. No flashes of light, no pain and destruction. Nothing. God had just smiled slightly and left. One moment He was there and the next gone. Gabriel had no idea where He had gone. After all, He was the Creator. He could have gone anywhere. It was something that nagged at him constantly. God had grown weak, but Gabriel had still expected a fight of some sort. But God's quiet surrender was more disturbing than the expected

battle for power. In a way, and to most of the other angels, it appeared as if what Gabriel had been saying all along were true. God had grown weak. Too weak to fight. Too weak to care. So he had simply left.

Gabriel liked to believe this, but something told him it wasn't true. So he must be prepared. He had established a tight security on the borders of Heaven. He had sent messengers to the angels battling for souls. For them to come home and help defend Heaven from any future attack—any attempt at reclamation of the throne by God. Lucifer could have the souls, he was getting them anyway. Let him build his tribute to himself. Arrogant bastard. At least that would keep him busy and he wouldn't feel the need to meddle in the affairs of Heaven.

Gabriel stood and moved to the balcony of the throne room and looked out upon Heaven. Beautiful in every sense—especially now that all the souls had been gathered and banished to the plains of Purgatory. He thought of the cesspool that the humans had turned their world into. "God's blessed children," Gabriel said with contempt. Let them wallow in their own filth and then go to Hell to continue doing the same thing they had done all their miserable lives. Let Lucifer build his world with the human vermin. Heaven would be pure and not bear the taint of humanity.

Gabriel stood on the balcony of the highest point in Heaven. Its beauty almost made him cry. But he shook it

# THE SLEEPERS AWAKEN

off and thought about the future. And he thought about…

A rustling behind him brought Gabriel out of his thoughts. Zaliel had come into the room with a dire look upon his face. Gabriel knew what it meant and he knew this would come. Zaliel nodded to Gabriel, "He's coming."

"I know," Gabriel said, turning back to the window. *I knew he would,* he thought.

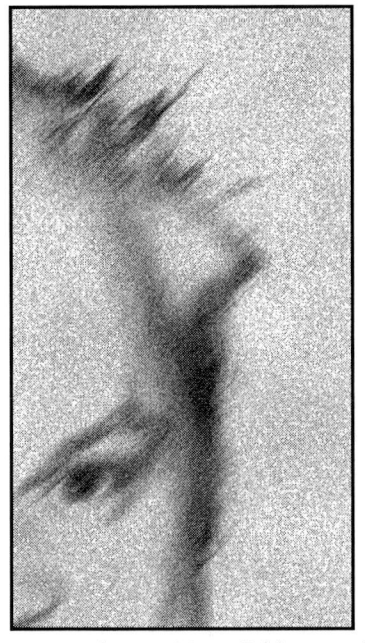

DAVE BARNETT lives on the outskirts of Orlando, Florida with his blind dachshund named Chauncey. During the day he works as a graphic designer for his Fat Cat Design company designing books for lots of small press publishers. At night he becomes DJ L.D. and runs Necropolis, a long-running industrial / EBM / synthpop / electro night at The Independent Bar in downtown Orlando.

Somewhere in there he has managed to run Necro Publications for the past 15 years, publishing some of the best names in modern horror: Edward Lee, Charlee Jacob, Gerard Houarner, Mehitobel Wilson, Jeffrey Thomas, Patrick Lestewka and dozens of others in various anthologies.

Dave has been published in a couple of the *Shivers* anthologies from Cemetery Dance Publications. He also has a story in the two-author chapbook *The Baby* along with Edward Lee. His collection, *Dead Souls*, came out form from Shocklines Press in 2004 and at least a couple of people seemed to like it.

*The Fallen: Book 1* is the first in what will hopefully be a long series books containing tales about angels and demons that will finally come together (fingers crossed) in one climatic battle for Heaven.

You can visit his official site at:
www.evilwriter.com

Also check out Dave's online DJ stuff:
necropodcast.podbean.com
www.clubnecropolis.com